MURDER ME!

ALSO BY MAX BRAND

The Dr. Kildare Series
Destry Rides Again
and approximately 218 other books, mysteries, westerns,
and short story collections in both genres

MURDER ME!

❖

Max Brand

St. Martin's Press
New York

Library of Congress Cataloging-in-Publication Data

Brand, Max, 1892-1944.
    Murder me! / Max Brand.
          p.   cm.
    "A Thomas Dunne book."
    ISBN 0-312-13569-6
    1. Police—New York (N.Y.)—Fiction.   I. Title.
PS3511.A87M79   1995
813'.52—dc20   95-23540
                                                    CIP

First Edition: November 1995

10   9   8   7   6   5   4   3   2   1

TABLE OF CONTENTS

MURDER ME!

1

❖

"The Man Who Wanted
to Die"

The letter asked for haste, but Willett always hurried with
a calm face. All the way from New York his car hit the
rain like a fist, knocking it into a dazzle before the headlights,
while Willett lounged at ease behind the wheel. When the
road was straight, it had a winter look, a black, polished river
that flowed under the wheels without carrying the machine
back; but, when the lights swung around a corner, they gave
him reassuring glimpses of spring, a horn of abundance, filled
with the bright rush of the rain, but with the summer green
about to flow into it.

He kept the thought in his mind, dreaming over it. Headlights twinkled, swayed up and down the hills, glared in his
face, and then went by with a thin squeal of tires or the roar of
a truck. He was off the main road and finding his way by instinct. Qualms of doubt made him sit up straighter. He had not
come this way for five years.

Then the lights showed him the old mill down by the creek,
trying to hide in the rain. He knew he was right from the
point. The side road carried him under a wet shimmer of trees.
At the turn he saw Telford's house. A pair of high-shouldered
wings had been added to his memory of it; but, of course,
Telford had prospered. He was the type. Afterwards, the lights
wavered across Barry's home, steadied on it, looked into the
familiar face. He slid the car up the oval of the gravel drive,
stopped, turned off the engine, switched on the curb lights.

The rain patted the top of the car with rapid little hands.

He got out and stretched. The trees that embosomed the place had grown smaller—because he had been taking long steps in the past five years, no doubt. There was one other change. An iron lantern hanging from the cornice above the door showed the way to the entrance. In the old days, oil lamps had been good enough for David Barry; electricity had been the mechanical slave and curse of man. It was Telford, no doubt, who had changed the mind of the old philanthropist. Willett rang the bell. In the pause, he listened to the rustling of the ampelopsis leaves; there was a smell of fresh paint.

The door opened a crack, jangling against a chain.

"Who's there?" asked David Barry.

"It's I, David."

"Ah, you," said Barry, and opened the door wide. The interior was dim. The lantern outside was what cast the shadow of big Willett over Barry, leaving only the pallor of his face and the sheen of his glasses. He shook hands, closing the door at the same time and saying, "You've grown bigger. That's a trick of imagination, I know, but the fancy is never wrong, entirely. Yes, you're a bigger man than you used to be. This way, Richard."

Willett dropped the weight of his overcoat, put up his hat, and had a glimpse of his face in the mirror. Some of the Eastern sleek had been rubbed off his cheekbones, some of the Nevada brown had been added. Perhaps that was why he looked bigger. He went behind Barry into the living room. There was a vase filled with such a spreading mass of spring bloom that it gave the place a busy air, like conversation.

"How does this old house seem to you?" asked Barry.

"You've always been so interested in doing good that you had to do good to a barn and turn it into a house," said Willett.

"You don't like it?"

"It must have been a good barn, but now it's faked. Those curved beams, for instance, are the bunk. Then you set in a carved overmantel of old English oak above the fireplace, like a bit of church choir installed in the stable. You open out one

2

wall and make a library balcony up there with Moorish columns and a French balustrade. You put Persian rugs on the floor, Chinese vases on the tables, and ring in this dash of Chinese sculpture."

He sunned his back at the fire and lighted a cigarette.

"You've turned æsthete, Richard, have you," said Barry. "You ought to know that all things which are truly beautiful may stand shoulder to shoulder."

Willett smoked and said nothing.

"This statue, for instance, is a Bodhisattva. It's a T'ang," explained Barry.

"Looks like a dancing girl with a prop smile to me," said Willett. "No, I'm not an æsthete."

"But like all our countrymen, you have a right to your own opinions, eh?"

Willett said nothing.

"A remarkable thing about our civilization," said Barry. "Without culture, without knowledge, we still express ourselves. Of course that is because we are so free . . . and so equal. The patriarch Jefferson and the puling French philosophers of the eighteenth century made us equal."

Willett said: "You talk the way you've always talked, but you look sick. What's the matter with you?"

"You're a mining engineer, now, Richard, and I dare say that you have undeveloped millions in prospect?"

"I won't talk business with you. I finished that five years ago when you handed over your affairs to Telford."

"What would you do for a hundred thousand dollars, Richard?"

"Murder," said Willett.

"That's why I sent for you," said Barry. "This morning I put you in my will for a hundred thousand dollars."

"The hell you did," answered Willett.

Something that was not a smile pulled at the corners of the mouth of Barry. He went to the long table, pulled open a drawer, and took thick, folded paper from it.

"You can see for yourself," said Barry.

3

"I'll take your word. You've always been afraid to tell a lie."

"Here is a loaded gun, Richard. Here am I. My servants come by the day, only. We are entirely alone. You have not been here for five years. No one could suspect your coming. In ten seconds the thing is finished and you are on the road again."

"Barring Telford, there's no one I'd rather put a bullet through than you," said Willett.

"I knew that, of course. I've understood for a long time . . . even when you were working for me . . . that you despised me, though I never knew why," Barry said.

"I hate a four-flusher who buys applause," said Willett. "You've always bought it. You've paid millions to get head-lines about the great-hearted philanthropist."

"There's the gun, Richard, and here am I."

"I think you're trying to be noble even now. How much have you left?"

"Between four and five million."

"Is that all?"

"I've been badly advised, Richard."

"I told you Telford would be a bust. Who gets the rest?"

"Jacqueline."

"Spindle-shanked little Jacqueline, eh? Does she give a damn about you?"

Barry said nothing. A slight color stained his cheeks. Hate steadied the eyes with which he looked at Willett.

"Let me have a drink, will you?" asked Willett.

"There on the sideboard. Help yourself."

Willett went to the decanter and sloshed some whiskey into a glass. He tossed it off neat.

"Even your Scotch is a fake," he said, and went back to the fireplace and a second cigarette. "What's the jam you're in?"

"I'm talking to you about a hundred thousand dollars. That's reason enough for you."

"You're afraid, all right," said Willett. "You're brittle and sick with fear. Tell me what the jam is."

4

Barry slipped into a chair. His head shuddered as he let it sink back against the cushion.

"I went into the contracting business," he said. "I was poorly advised, Richard. Before certain city contracts could be secured, money had to change hands . . . and Telford has just found out that the district attorney is going to start an investigation tomorrow."

"Philanthropist accused of bribery and corruption, eh? That would be sweet! I'd love that," said Willett, and laughed.

Barry closed his eyes. Willett brought him three fingers of whiskey.

"Take a shot of this," he directed.

The glass tinkled against the teeth of Barry. His head wavered as he lifted it. After one swallow he began to cough and writhe a little.

"It's rotten stuff, right enough," agreed Willett, and finished off the drink. "But that ought to brace you a little. Who's the district attorney?"

"Thomas Hunt Lawlor."

"I know that bird and he's as crooked as a dog's hind leg. Can't Telford get to him?"

"Lawlor aims at being governor," said Barry. He put his head in his hands. "Richard, if I'm not dead before morning, I will burn that will and you lose a hundred thousand dollars. Did you tell anyone you were coming out here?"

"Not a soul."

"Then the way is open to you."

"Why don't you put the gun to your crooked head and pull the trigger? Burn the will, and shoot yourself, and save a hundred thousand for dear little buck-toothed Jacqueline. I'll stand here and watch the body fall for old time's sake. Head's up, David. I've always given you good advice. There won't be any pain. Just lay the muzzle against the temple and pull the trigger and you'll be laid away with your headlines; the district attorney will never bark up a dead tree, and somebody will build you a monument, somewhere."

5

"I tried poison," said Barry, "and my lips would not let it pass. I tried a gun and the cold of the steel . . . I tried gas, but when the tube was in my mouth. . . ."

He leaped out of his chair.

"Now, steady, steady!" said Willett. "Don't be a damned fool."

"Oh my God, oh my God!" said Barry.

"Sit down," commanded Willett. "Have you got a telephone?"

"No. I wouldn't have . . . the babble of the crowd. . . ."

"Very well. I'm going out to find one and have a little think."

"What good will the telephone be? What can you do? Richard, don't leave me alone!"

"Do I care if you sweat for another hour?" demanded Willett. "Take your scrawny hands off me!"

In the hall he paused to put on his coat and hat. He drew on his gloves before he touched the knob of the front door.

2

❖

"Shadows That Creep"

I t was more than an hour later when Willett sat again at the fire of David Barry, smoking, blowing up the smoke, looking carefully through the brown mist toward the dead man. Barry hung by the neck with a doubled curtain-cord tied about his throat. The cord was fastened to the balustrade of the library gallery. He was still swaying—the force in a pendulum runs down so slowly—and the movement stirred slightly the silver of his lifted hair. This gave him a touch of life. His face held a slightly sardonic grin and his head, twisted to the side, added an air of thought.

Willett tossed the butt into the fire and stood up, pulled on his gloves. It was when he was standing that he noticed, for the first time, a little riffle of white that lay at the foot of one of the legs of the long table. He picked up a woman's handkerchief. The linen was so delicate that the slightest breath of air would have been enough to keep it floating. The perfume was hardly noticeable—merely a clean fragrance. Willett looked toward the dead man. Hardly more than a hundred and twenty pounds in that starved body, he estimated. Then he slid the handkerchief into his pocket. The big automatic on the table he put away in his clothes also.

From a small table near the fire he took a newspaper, carried a hard-bottomed chair to the pendulous body of Barry, laid the paper on the seat of the chair and stepped up. His face was now almost on a level with that of Barry. He dusted his gloves against his clothes, opened his coat, rubbed them once more against his white shirt. After that he untied Barry's necktie. It was a hand-woven silk, blue, with small gray-white flowers worked into the pattern. He looked at this for a moment, repassed it around Barry's neck, and tied it again with care, adding touches like a woman before a mirror.

Stepping down from the chair, he returned it to its place, tossed the newspaper into the fire, and watched the roar of flame jump up the chimney. Some small, withering flakes of gray ash showered down onto the hearth. He brushed them back with the hearth broom and looked again at the corpse, critically. Something about it was not to his taste, so he returned and, this time, untied and tied again the laces of the dangling shoes. When he had finished this, he noticed that the body had stopped swinging. With a push he restarted the gentle oscillation. After that, he went into the adjoining bedroom.

A heavy wooden four-poster looked too big for the chamber. The head was toward a recessed window. There was a fireplace fitted with a paneled door, a small built-in bookcase that made a pleasant spot of color in the rough plaster of the wall; figured chintz framed the two windows. A soft tan rug covered the floor.

Willett stepped behind the bed and pulled hard on the head posts. The bed gave way slowly toward him. He pushed it back in place and noticed that the casters had left distinct trails across the nap of the rug. There was not a solid headboard but fluted wooden balusters which would have the advantage of letting light from the window pour over the shoulder of one who wished to read in bed. Barry had that habit. On the bedside table were Florence Ayscough's three volumes of translations from the Chinese, a paper cutter, a fountain pen desk set, an ashtray of pale jade. Willett took off the bedcover, folded it, laid it across the back of a chair. Under the pillow he found a fresh suit of pajamas, white silk with heavy blue embroidery around the buttonholes. He took off his shoes, pulled on the pajamas, opened the bed, and got into it. He lighted a cigarette from the box of them on the bedside table and opened one of the Ayscough books.

Tu Fu was a great poet but sad, aching with sadness. Willett tamped out the cigarette. Jabbing the coal down against the polish of the jade was a desecration. He replaced the book on the table, open and face down, got up from the bed, took off the pajamas and looked at his clothes to make sure that no white threads had adhered to them. Next there was the smoothing of the pillows, the replacing of the carefully folded pajamas under them, the remaking of the bed, the replacing of the cover. It was hard to do these things with gloved hands.

As he finished, the wind leaped out of the whistling distance and struck the house, shaking it till the windows hummed and the shutters rattled. A long, hushing draught ran through the place as though a door had been opened.

Willett pulled the automatic out of his pocket and raised his eyes to listen. The breathing of the wind ceased through the house; it went roaring off among the trees. A taint of wood smoke had entered the air from the living room.

He stepped into the adjoining bedroom. He himself had used that bed more than once in the other days. He remembered even the figures in the design of the toile de Jouy that curtained the little, high windows. The same cloth covered the chairs beside the fireplace, and there was a pillar lamp on the fireside table exactly like that in Barry's room, except that the shade was red. He started a little when he saw this, then took the shade from the lamp and passed back into the other chamber. The shade of Barry's bedside light was drum-shaped and an appropriate green with a little Directoire print on one side. He removed that shade also and deliberately toppled the standard to the ground. The crash of the fall was surprisingly loud. His muscles jumped. He had to set his teeth and, when he leaned to pick up the fallen lamp, he started about, suddenly. A shadow seemed to be disappearing to the left of the living room door. But that was nerves, of course.

Rather pale, now, his head jutting forward with strain, he examined the standard of the lamp. A bit of the gilding had broken away from the painted base; that was all. He put on the lamp the shade he had taken from the adjoining bedchamber and went back into the living room. To cross the threshold took effort. A faint swirl of smoke and ashes from the hearth hung like a ghost in the air. David Barry, his head thoughtfully on one side, his eyes half-closed, meditated upon him. Willett dropped the Directoire shade into the fire. It was gone in a gust of flame. With the tongs he picked the wire frame out of the fire and put it to one side.

Still there was something to do in the back of the house. He returned through Barry's chamber into the bathroom. When he snapped on the light, it polished the white of the tiles. All was in undisturbed order, particularly the linen hand towels on the swinging rack beside the washbowl. It would have been a stupid oversight to leave this place untouched.

Another burst of storm went racketing overhead and whistling underfoot. In the mirror before him he saw his face was bright with sweat. His eyes were too big.

He washed his hands, dried them on a towel, replaced it on the rack. From the cabinet behind the mirror he took a tube of toothpaste, unscrewed the top from it, left it on the glass shelf below the mirror. There was a toothbrush, the bristles a little ragged toward the toe. He moistened that brush and placed it beside the tube of paste.

Everything was finished now, if he could get safely from the house. An invincible fear slid his hand down to the butt of the automatic as he opened the door of the bathroom. Again, shadows seemed to shrink swiftly away to either side. Nerves once more. He rubbed the back of his chamois glove across his sweating lips. His eyes were stretched so wide open they ached.

So across the threshold of the living room again. He got the wire frame from the hearth, crumpled it, tucked it into a pocket. He walked on. The body of David Barry was beside him, behind him, no longer moving with a pendulous sway but slowly turning to this side and then to that. Now the eyes were directly behind him, watching with perfect indifference, with perfect knowledge.

He jerked open the door to the entrance hall and fairly leaped through into it. But then he remembered something else. He had to turn about and look at Barry again before he

10

reached for the switch and snapped the room into darkness. Through the black shadow, something ran at him on swift tiptoes.

He set his teeth and waited, leaning forward a little. If a man gives way every time his nerves go haywire, he'll break up quickly. The tiptoe rush out of darkness came straight at him, ceased, went over his shoulder in a mild breath of air.

Willett closed the door then. He refused to look at himself in the hall mirror as he put on his coat and hat. Now as he leaned at the front door, his hand on the knob of it, another man was leaning on the farther side in exactly the same posture.

Nerves again! He jerked the door open with a sudden decision—and saw before him the face of the wild outer night. Stars were in the west with clouds rolling back from them in masses, stained low down by the glare of the city lights.

He looked into his car before he climbed under the wheel. The self-starter labored, paused, labored again. If the car would not run, could he push it forward to the next incline of the highway? He knew that he could not. He tried the self-starter again. This time the eight cylinders began firing with a purr that was much too loud.

In the quiet night of a city one could hear the noise of a starting engine half a mile away; but here there was the friendly uproar of the wind.

At last he was gliding down the driveway, lurching over the dip of the gutter onto the road. Fifty miles an hour was standing still. Sixty, seventy meant nothing. He hit eighty-five before fear began to blow away behind him. A few deep breaths set his heart right. He slowed to seventy; he could have dropped to forty if he chose, for the thing was entirely behind him. Time was like that—first a nothingness, then the impenetrable solidity of a wall.

The headlights flickered across dense brush beside the road. He screwed down the right-hand window and flung away the little tangled knot of the wire frame.

His hotel was too big to have a brain. He got the key to his room and went up in the elevator wondering what it was that depressed him with a near sense of trouble. Not until he was in his room did he remember the big automatic and the handkerchief, but between him and the house of David Barry now extended winding miles of rain-washed road, the pause and pouring of the city traffic, the mindless preoccupation of this great hotel.

He put the handkerchief and the gun into the top drawer of the dresser, well behind his collars and ties. Tomorrow he would manage to dispose of them both.

3

❖

"In a Dark Room"

Detective Sergeant Angus Campbell was only thirty-two but already he was so bald that his head was varnished with highlights. He had big, bald eyes also, meaningless except when they began to glare with anger. They were glaring now as he fingered his telephone a moment before lifting it from the hook.

"Give me Detective Sergeant Patrick O'Rourke," he said, and waited.

The family of Angus Campbell came from western Scotland; he himself came from western Nebraska. Like all his people, he was tall, erect, lean, and he carried his shoulders so square that a chip could be kept in balance on each of them. He had a gray, sober, sad face framed by a pair of great ears, red, outjutting, somewhat hairy. He had come to New York a dozen years before to become a reporter but, when he discovered that reporters only skim the surface of things, he joined the police. Angus Campbell was thorough.

A drawling voice spoke over the wire.

"This is Angus Campbell," said the sergeant.

"Seems to me I've heard of you before," answered Sergeant O'Rourke.

Campbell gritted his teeth.

"The inspector," said Campbell, "has assigned us together on another case."

"Who? You and me? He can't assign us on another. I resign. I wouldn't. . . ."

13

"Resign and be damned," said Angus Campbell, and hung up the telephone.

But he was not surprised to find himself, after that bright moment of hope, once more in the back of a police car with O'Rourke, once more with the stench of an O'Rourke cigar making his nostrils pinch together. He never looked at O'Rourke when he could avoid it but, when he was with the Irishman, the picture of that red, gross face came between him and his work, possessed his mind, made all his nerves taut.

Sergeant Campbell kept his wife and two children in a walk-up on 125th Street. Sergeant O'Rourke managed a Lexington Avenue apartment and his family summered in the cool green of Connecticut.

"As long as the inspector has rubbed our noses in it again," said O'Rourke, "why not take it like men? Why not talk? The quicker we use the bean and solve this job, the quicker we can say good-bye."

Disgust pressed the lips of Angus Campbell close together; an irresistible sense of logic parted them again.

"Aye," said he.

"Take a fellow like this David Barry, with three volumes of newspaper clippings and five million berries on the bush, why should he dive off the balcony and choke himself?" asked O'Rourke.

"There's nothing surprising about what a philanthropist does," said Angus Campbell, "not once he's started being a philanthropist."

"Sometimes they got a past to bury," said O'Rourke.

"Mostly it's a future that they want to get," answered Campbell.

"There would be motives for the murder, if it's a murder," said O'Rourke. "The will, one day old, was found in the drawer of the table in the room where old Barry hung. It leaves a hundred thousand dollars to a fellow by name of Richard Willett, a mining engineer just back in New York a couple of days. It leaves all the rest of the millions to his nearest relative, a gal by name of Jacqueline Barry, a free spender. The dress-makers in Paris begin to eat when she arrives. She's loaded with debts; she's five-feet-eight inches, a hundred-and-thirty-odd, rides in the first flight, and a good forehand drive . . . an all-round girl, she is, says the inspector. There's Barry's partner in the contracting business, Jeff Morrison, that never done any-body but Big Jeff any good. That's three to look at. Have a cigar, Angus?"

"I never smoke till I can afford a good one," said Campbell.

He was so pleased by this remark that he looked out the window and enjoyed that swift green rolling of the landscape, new-washed by the rain and shining now in the sun.

"God forgive Himself for making a man like you!" said O'Rourke. And they were silent the rest of the way to the Barry house.

Automobiles filled the entire oval of the entrance drive. A weary-faced lieutenant of police met them and gave his report.

"We've kept the newspapers in the dark. That's a break for you boys," he pointed out. "Medical examiner says that it's death by strangulation. No tap on the head or anything. Straight suicide, but the inspector wants it looked into. Tele-phoned to Mr. Jeffrey Morrison, Barry's partner in the con-tracting business. . . . Meet Detective Sergeants Campbell and O'Rourke, Mr. Morrison."

He had an alderman's bulk set on the legs of an athlete, a pink face, soft, hairy, pink hands. He held a cigar fishtailed into a wide, wet mass by much chewing.

"Glad to meet you boys," said Jeffrey. "I hope you dig into this. David Barry . . . well, all I say is: Why? Why? Man revered by the whole world . . . and so, why? is all I say."

"Who's the red-haired whiz-bang in the car, there, lieuten-ant?" asked O'Rourke.

"That's the heiress. There's five million dollars between her and yesterday. Miss Jacqueline Barry. . . . Meet Detective Ser-geants O'Rourke and Campbell."

She said how-do-you-do to them without smiling. They went on.

15

"Cool," said O'Rourke. "Cool as hell, but I always go for green eyes. Have a cigar, lieutenant? Who's the big bird with the jaw and the eye?"

"Mr. Richard Willett, meet Detective Sergeants Campbell and O'Rourke. They'll take charge of the investigation, Mr. Willett. And Mr. John Telford. We telephoned to Telford and Miss Barry. Telford's the neighbor and lawyer of David Barry," explained the lieutenant. "The woman sitting under the tree, crying, is Matilda Grunsky. She's the servant. She found the body."

"She's not crying because she cares," said Sergeant Campbell. "She's only crying because she thinks she ought to. Is everything the same inside?"

"The body's been removed to the bedroom. Can't leave a dead man swinging all day. It kind of offends people, somehow."

"You telephoned to the rest. Why's Willett here?" asked O'Rourke.

"He got a letter from Barry asking him to come out in a rush. I saw the letter. It's all in order."

"Why the rush?" asked Campbell.

"Why a dead man, either?" asked the lieutenant. "How do I know why the rush? You boys come in, now? The rest of you folks just wait out here a few minutes and then you can all come inside."

They passed into the living room.

"That's where he hung from," said the lieutenant. "I left the curtain cord hanging right there. No sign up there in the balcony. . . . Hanging there, his feet half a yard off the floor, cooked. The medical examiner says something like ten o'clock last night. Around about there. There's the will on the table. . . ."

"Five million, besides what he wasted, you'd think he would of blown himself to a better dump than this," said O'Rourke.

Campbell trailed behind, using his eyes. O'Rourke seemed to have no need of eyes. He trusted the lieutenant.

16

They went into the bedroom.

"Peaceful, ain't he?" said O'Rourke, admiringly. "Can't you close his eyes?"

"Not yet and keep them closed," said the lieutenant. "Look the whole show over, boys. Why the hell the inspector wanted to drag you all the way out here for nothing I can't tell. Shall I let the others in?"

"Sit down a minute and let 'em think we're doing our stuff," said O'Rourke. "Sit down, Campbell. There's nothing to find here but suicide and the moral lesson."

"There's one queer one," said the lieutenant. "The old boy always used to carry three or four thousand around in his pocket. He's been known to stop bang in the middle of the street and pass a cold thousand to one of the poor and deserving. But there's no spot cash in his pocket now. There's not even a wallet."

Angus Campbell said, "You'd be meaning that a thief strangled him and then dropped the body over the balcony railing, yonder? Would a thief waste the time to do that after he once had the money in his pocket?"

"Logical is what old Angus is," said O'Rourke. "He don't believe in fish till after he's swallered it. You could let in the crowd now. I guess our day's work is done."

They entered the house talking quietly, but not at all sadly, together. Tall, handsome John Telford walked first with Jacqueline Barry. Morrison and Willett came in the rear. They passed into the bedroom.

Angus Campbell, standing with O'Rourke at the doorway, could not help observing, "Not a tear in the lot of them. They're all modern. Lawyer, partner, heiress, legatee, and not a wet eye in the lot. Too modern to feel any emotion. Machines. Detectives used to have a chance. They could read faces. But now we might as well look at monkeys. You take a widow at noon and she grieves till it's cocktail time, unless somebody drops in for tennis in the afternoon."

John Telford exclaimed suddenly: "What's the matter, Jacqueline? Here . . . we'll get to some air."

17

He half-carried her past the detectives, her head on his shoulder. In a chair under the living room window he placed her.

"Listen!" muttered Campbell. "That's modern, isn't it?"

She was saying: "Sorry, John. I didn't think it would hit me so hard. We never cared a rap for each other. If his eyes had been closed, it would have been all right."

The voice of Richard Willett said, "I didn't know that Barry was color-blind. What's a red lamp shade doing in this room?"

"What's the matter with it? It looks all right to me," said O'Rourke.

"Wait a minute," said Campbell. "Lieutenant!"

"Well?" asked the policeman.

"That light in the living room . . . that wasn't touched? Nobody switched it off?"

"No," said the lieutenant. "What you driving at?"

"Speaking of lamps is what made me think," admitted Campbell. "Maybe the light's burned out."

He strode across the living room and turned the switch. The shades of the floor lamps brightened. "You sure nobody touched the switch since Barry's body was found?" he demanded.

"I'll get the maid and ask her," said the lieutenant.

She came with great eyes, walking as though the floor were thin ice.

"When you came in here this morning," said Campbell, "did you touch the electric switch by the door?"

"I only seen," said Matilda Grunsky, "and then I didn't touch anything."

"Come across with it," said O'Rourke. "Everybody's looking at you, Angus. What's the matter with you?"

"Well," said Campbell, "I was only thinking it was a queer thing that a man would commit suicide in the dark."

"Well, damn my eyes, I'm a fool!" said O'Rourke.

He looked toward the girl. She was sitting up straight in her chair, suddenly, and instead of staring at the brightness of the lamps, she was looking across the room toward the curtain cord

18

that still dangled from the balcony in two long strands, significantly curled up at the ends.

John Telford said: "No, that's true!"

Big Jeffrey Morrison exclaimed: "That's what I said. Lieutenant, you remember I said it: Why? Why should he do it? I tell you, it's going to turn out murder. Would a man climb all the way up onto that balcony and tie the rope around his neck and the other end around the railing and then jump? What would he be trying to do? Save the electric bill? You can see what a trained mind does. *You* have the trained mind, Sergeant Campbell."

O'Rourke shifted his gaze to Richard Willett. The man with the jaw and the eye had not spoken a word. He was lighting a cigarette, carefully, like a man untroubled by thought.

4

❖

"The Murderer Is
Color-Blind"

"Anybody's eyes is as good as the next man's if he uses them," said O'Rourke. "Trained, my foot! Mr. Willett, you're not a painter or something, are you? Then tell me what's wrong with this red lamp shade."

"But it shouldn't be there!" cried Matilda Grunsky. "It belongs in the next room. Right in there . . . why, it was there last night and now there's nothing on that lamp."

"What was on this lamp by the bed?" asked O'Rourke.

"A green shade with a queer picture on it of ladies. . . ."

"Where's the shade now?"

"I don't know."

"Find it," said O'Rourke. "Everybody, find the green lamp shade. . . ."

"Here's a green one right in the living room. What about this?"

"That's different," declared Matilda Grunsky. "The picture on it's different."

They found no green lamp shade.

"I don't see that it's anything of importance," said Willett. "How could it be?"

"Let me see this lamp," said O'Rourke. "Is it new or old?"

"New, sir," said Matilda.

"Why's the gilding off, here?"

"It can't be off," said Matilda. "I dust it every day and . . . what *has* happened to it?"

"It fell on the floor," said O'Rourke. "Here's the mark where it hit the paint. Wait a minute . . . here's a speck of the gilding. Now, who knocked that lamp off the table? It's not near the way to the bathroom. Anybody lie down on this bed for a snooze, yesterday?"

"Mr. Barry never lies down in the day, sir. I've never known him to."

"Who knocked over the lamp, if he wasn't lying down on the bed? Who smoked the cigarette that's here in the tray?" demanded Campbell.

"Lord in heaven knows that I cleaned the tray yesterday morning!" declared Matilda Grunsky. "Ah, *what* do you mean? Why are you looking at me?"

"Shut up and stop your yammering," directed O'Rourke. "You cleaned the tray in the morning. The chief never lies down in the day. But somebody puts a cigarette in the tray; somebody knocks the lamp over, somebody changes the green shade for the red, and then eats the green one. Saying anything, Campbell?"

"We'll put Mr. Barry on the couch."

They carried the body to the couch and stretched it out there. Campbell took the cover from the bed.

"How fresh are the sheets on the bed?" asked O'Rourke.

"Two days, sir."

"They won't tell us much, then. But somebody was lying on this bed yesterday . . . yesterday in the evening after Matilda, here, goes home."

He lifted the pillows.

"The blue is kind of a neat idea, eh?" said O'Rourke, lifting the pajamas. "How often had he slept in these?"

"Never, sir. I put them out right fresh, yesterday. Mr. Barry is kind of finicky about wrinkled pajamas. . . ."

"Then what are all these wrinkles doing in them?" asked O'Rourke.

He spread the pajamas on the bed. Matilda was stunned.

"Cheer up, sweetheart," said O'Rourke. "Nobody thinks that *you* slept in 'em. Back up everybody, will you? I need air."

The silent group looking on from the doorway moved slightly. O'Rourke tossed the pajamas aside. Campbell took the covers from one side and O'Rourke from the other. One by one they turned them down over the foot of the bed with Matilda looking on carefully. The upper sheet went back in white ripple before she cried out: *"I* never made that bed! Look at the wrinkles coming all up into that corner! *I* never made the bed that way."

The detectives looked at one another.

"Take the gentlemen and the lady outside, if you please, Lieutenant. We'll just keep Matilda."

The lieutenant escorted the rest from the house.

"Go on," said O'Rourke. "Do your stuff. Get logical!"

Campbell glared at him, but presently he said, "I undress, put on my pajamas, get into bed. . . . When did Mr. Barry go to bed?"

"Any time after nine, sir."

". . . into bed, light a cigarette, read a book . . . this book here . . . and all at once I've knocked over the lamp. Or maybe when I open the bed I knock the lamp over, go into the next room, get a new shade, and put the green shade that's been broken . . . no, O'Rourke, it doesn't work."

"You're damn right it doesn't work," said O'Rourke. "This is gonna be good, Angus. This is gonna be a honey. Oh, my God, what a honey this is gonna be!"

"The man who took the green shade off the lamp afterwards destroyed it," said Campbell.

"Sure," agreed O'Rourke. "Because the thing was knocked out of shape and might of started people asking questions and looking around the bed. The poor dummy didn't realize that he was putting a red shade in here for a green one. Now, what happened? Was Barry in that bed, last night? He was. The pajamas was slept in. And in that bed he was strangled! That's it. But how could a murderer walk in while the mug stays there in bed and waits to be killed?"

"It was a friend, Pat. He's lying in bed. A ring comes at the door. He goes and lets in an old friend. He knows the caller.

22

Asks him in and comes back out of the cold and climbs into bed. That's easy. He wouldn't notice if his friend walked around behind his back. The next thing he notices . . . look, through the bars here at the head of the bed, the curtain cord is looped through and pulled around his neck a good, hard tug "

"Oh, mother of heaven!" breathed Matilda Grunsky.

"Here! Look here!" said O'Rourke. "When you clean up the room, do you push this bed around, Matilda?"

"I never do that more than once in six months," said Matilda.

"Ah, ha!" said O'Rourke. "But notice this, Angus. Where the wheels have run back towards the window. You can see the tracks where they were pushed forward again, too. Why, it's all easy. And afterwards, the crook dresses the dead body, makes up the bed, changes the lamp shade . . . because, while he was being strangled, Barry has given the lamp a kick . . . and afterwards the killer carries or drags Barry up onto the library balcony and hangs him from the railing. Isn't that a straight story? A straight story of a fellow with a long head and no nerves."

Campbell, without answering, walked past the staring face of Matilda Grunsky, and leaned over the body of Barry. He untied the necktie.

"You're right, Pat," he announced. "You see? A man ties his own necktie with the thin end on the left. If he tied it on another fellow, he'd keep the thin end in the same left hand, but that brings it on the right side of the other man's neck. That's what you see here. Barry was murdered in bed, dressed, and hanged from the balcony. And that man was color-blind. . . . Matilda, go call in the people from the front of the house!"

5

"The Green Tie"

M orrison sat on the running board of his automobile, taking his cigar from his mouth and shaking his head disapprovingly, from time to time. If anyone came near him he would say: "Why? That's what I said in the first place? Why *would* he?" So no one came near Morrison. Telford and Jacqueline Barry walked slowly up and down until Willett went to them.

"You haven't forgotten me, Jacqueline, have you?" he asked. "Telford would keep my memory ripe; wouldn't you, John?"

"He keeps your memory fresh and new," said the girl. "Why do you two hate each other so thoroughly?"

They regarded one another with calm eyes of detestation.

"There's nothing better than a good aged-in-the-wood hatred," said Willett. "It clears the brain, sharpens the eyes; it's the mustard on the roast beef and the salt on the egg. You're engaged, you two, aren't you?"

"That's right." The girl nodded. She gave all her attention to Willett, which seemed to put her entirely on the side of Telford.

"Then I can be frank," exclaimed Willett. "Even when we went to school together, I hated his damned, handsome face. I was always tackle or guard. I made the holes in the line and the brilliant halfback flashed through them. Telford was the brilliant halfback."

"John has to have applause," agreed Jacqueline. Her green eyes flashed at him, and her smile.

24

Telford said with his soft voice and pleasant deliberation:

"I worked underground and got your uncle's legal business, Jacqueline. I got into his good graces and got Dick out."

"He never was in good graces," answered Jacqueline. "Were you, Richard? You and Uncle David always were snarling at one another. Isn't it a bit easy for you to hate people?"

"Very easy," said Willett.

"Ah, but when he doesn't hate . . . ," murmured Telford.

"He brings all the devil to the top of you, doesn't he, John?" observed the girl, watching Telford with an almost maternal interest. "What are you doing now, Richard?"

"Mining engineering, when I can find a mine to engineer. You've changed a good deal."

She pointed to her mouth: "Teeth?"

"To begin with," said Willett. "You weren't a smiling sort of a girl, in those days."

"I was afraid of my teeth," she answered. "All I could do was to keep them white and under cover."

"That wasn't the only reason," said Willett. "There was Uncle David to poison the soup. I'd like to know you better before John carries you off. Shall I ask your permission, John?"

Telford said, "That's the Iago of it. Frank, open, manly, sincere, with the dagger up the sleeve. But go as far as you can, Dick."

"Thanks," said Willett, "I shall."

She looked quickly at him with a smile beginning, but then she saw that he was grave.

"He means it, John," she said.

"Dick is never the man to waste words," said Telford. "Never . . . damn him!"

"I think you two are only half a step from liking each other a lot," declared Jacqueline.

"Do you think that?" asked Willett, smiling. "Well, you're not very old, after all."

"If you will all come in, please," said Matilda Grunsky, at

the open door of the house. "The gentlemen want to see you all."

"What Campbell doesn't see, O'Rourke will smell," observed Willett on the way in. "I'd hate to have the pair of them on my trail."

"They'd have a lot of ground to cover," said Telford.

In the living room on the davenport near the fire were arranged a mass of neckties. The detectives stood by.

"Uncle David was always bright about his ties," said the girl.

"You simply didn't give a damn about him, did you?" asked Willett.

She looked slowly up toward the ceiling. "No," she decided. "Not a damn."

"Miss Barry," said Sergeant Campbell, "if you will kindly step to the couch and select a red tie and bring it to me. . . . Thank you. . . . Now, Mr. Willett, the same. . . . Thanks. . . . Mr. Morrison, a green tie. . . . Thank you. . . . Mr. Telford, if you please. A green tie, please. . . . Ah!"

For Telford had picked up carelessly a pair of red neckties and was offering them to the detective.

"Interesting," said Willett, in a clear voice.

"Are you color-blind, Mr. Telford?" asked O'Rourke.

"Dick!" cried the girl.

"What's the matter?" exclaimed Telford. "Color-blind? Why, I don't think so. . . ."

Campbell took the two ties and smoothed them.

Willett said, "My compliments, Sergeant Campbell. I was just saying that if Campbell couldn't see a rat, O'Rourke could smell it."

Campbell raised his hand. With his prominent eyes he stared at Telford.

"The man who murdered David Barry was color-blind, Mr. Telford," he said.

"The man who murdered him? Why, it was suicide!" said Telford. "Why, good heavens . . . color-blind . . . what are you talking about? Jacqueline. . . ."

She went to him and laid a hand on his arm, saying, "Be patient, John."

"Well?" demanded Campbell, turning suddenly on O'Rourke.

"Well, what of it?" asked O'Rourke. "We'll find out where they were last night. Any of you together? No?"

"I've got to find out what . . . ," began Telford.

"Let the sergeant and me do the finding out," said O'Rourke. "Where were you last night?"

"At home."

"That's just down the road, I understand?"

"Yes."

"You stayed in the whole evening?"

"Yes," said Telford. "Let me see . . . I think. . . . Yes, I was in the house all evening."

"Didn't step out for a breath of air?"

"It was raining cats and dogs. Why should I step out?"

O'Rourke said, "Well, Miss Barry. Where were you?"

"I drove over to Waterton and went to a movie."

"Alone?"

"That was why I went to the movie." She smiled.

"Mr. Morrison?"

"Who, me? Why, I . . . I was engaged all evening."

The big man turned from pink to crimson.

"Oh, you were engaged all evening, were you?" said O'Rourke. "Well, where?"

He stepped up close to Morrison and took his arm.

"In my car," said O'Rourke.

"You can see the girl if you have to," said Morrison, "but no infernal newspapers. Rose Taylor. I'll give you the address."

"We'll take a look into it later on, maybe," said O'Rourke. He added, "Mr. Willett?"

"I started out to make a tour of New York. The rain came down with a smash when I was close to an old speakeasy that I used to know. The Pêche d'Or. I went in there and found it legal and full."

"These here statements are all being taken down," O'Rourke said with a sudden loudness. "If any of you want to change your statements, this is the time to speak up. Go ahead and refresh your memories, all of you. We'll give you two minutes for that."

"Nothing more to say, all of you? Then, you're free to scatter. We want no more of you today," said O'Rourke.

He went over to Campbell.

"It's Telford," said O'Rourke. "But we can't grab him now."

"It's not Telford," said Campbell.

"Look," said O'Rourke. "Engaged to five millions, their keeper all alone every night. In a neighboring house, at that. Take a slant at the color-blind Telford. He's got the handsome face. Never knew a pretty man yet there wasn't some hell in him."

"It's not Telford," said Campbell.

"Who is it then, dummy?"

"Maybe the man that first used the word 'color-blind.' Back there in the bedroom, the first to see that the red lampshade was in the wrong room."

"Willett, you mean? You're cockeyed."

"One day," said Sergeant Campbell, "except for the wheeze in your lungs and the dirty fat that clogs up your belly and your face and your brain, I'd put hands on you when you call me another name, you Irish swine."

"Good!" said O'Rourke. "I like to hear you talk like this. The same as I like butter on my toast. One day I'm gonna break you open and eat your heart."

"Bah!" said Campbell. "Willett's the man to watch."

O'Rourke turned on his heel, breathing heavily.

6

❖

"The Alibi"

Telford said to his butler, "Even in summer weather, I want you to see that there's always plenty of wood for every fireplace, Murray. It blew up cold last night and I had to bring wood from the library into my study."

"I thought I filled the study woodbox just the other day, sir," said Murray.

"Well, it's true that I used a good deal, because I was in the study all evening. But watch the woodboxes, Murray."

"Very good, sir. Very sorry, sir."

"It's quite all right," said Telford.

"Where could we go tonight?" asked Jacqueline.

"You wouldn't be running out to a show tonight, Jacqueline, would you?"

"Because my uncle is dead? Why not? The whole world knows that we hated one another, and I won't be a hypocrite in black about his death. Where *could* we go? Is there a moving picture anywhere? Somewhere near, I mean?"

"Well, Waterton's the nearest. A silly thing called *The First Smile,* with Sue Maryland and Larry Lloyd in it."

"Anyway, I saw that last night," said Jacqueline. "And what a bore!"

La Pêche d'Or was crowded to the doors and the horseshoe bar in the center of the room was ringed with a double row of drinkers. Willett made his way in slowly.

"I'll get you one," said a lad at a corner table, rising. "What'll you have?"

And the girl answered, "Get me one of those fast ones that Sammy makes. . . . Second Chance, is what he calls it."

Willett drifted up to the bar.

"Evening, Sammy," he said.

"Good evening, sir," said Sammy, setting out glasses with one hand and working a shaker with the other.

"What was that drink you mixed for me last night?" asked Willett.

"When, sir?"

"Last night, about this time. 'Last Chance,' did you call it?"

"No, sir. Second Chance. Coming right up, sir."

WHEN JEFFREY MORRISON got back to his office, he always was assured of certain pleasures unusual to the business place of a downtown building contractor. In the corners of the waiting room bushy gardenias overflowed their great pots with a polished flood of green and with sweetness from the white blossoms; but in his own spacious private office, Morrison kept camellias, white and rose, fountain-shaped plants which bloomed all in a week and then were replaced by fresh perfections. Best of all, when Morrison wished to make a memorandum of the desire of some client, he pressed a bell and there came to him as secretary a girl so lovely that one glance at her proved the culture of her employer. Whenever she looked down at her notebook, she was beautifully serious and, when she looked up, she could not help smiling, so that one could see that she had a charming nature and delighted in her work.

Today, although there was no client in his office, as soon as he returned to it Jeffrey Morrison pressed the bell and Rose Taylor entered. Always when she entered she made, in the closing of the door behind her, what seemed a grave little bow, smiling as she straightened from it.

"Yes, Mr. Morrison," she said.

He looked toward both the doors and wished that they could be locked for a few minutes.

"Come here, Rose," he said.

"Yes, Mr. Morrison," she answered, and came to stand by his desk.

He said with a grin, "You're perfect at it, Rose."

"Thank you, Mr. Morrison," she said, lifting her eyes with her smile.

It disappeared again as she looked down once more.

"I've got something to talk to you about. Something serious," he said.

"Yes, Mr. Morrison," said Rose.

He kept his eyes on her as he took from his pocket a small case, opened it, and took out a ring set with a blue-white flame of big diamonds. This he slipped on one of her soft fingers which lifted, or seemed to lift, with an automatic intelligence to receive the gift.

"You ought to have that," said Morrison. "You're short on that kind of hardware."

He studied her face closely, always expecting a blush; it was the only respect in which she continually disappointed him.

"Thank you, Mr. Morrison," she said.

"If I didn't know that you were a good girl, Rose," he said, "I would . . . well, this is the point. I spent last evening with you."

"Did you, Mr. Morrison?"

"Listen . . . I mean it. I went up to your place and we had a quiet little dinner together. From seven to ten, say."

"Yes, Mr. Morrison," said she.

"I wish you would lay off the business manners for two minutes," he said. "But let that go. Wait a minute. I brought in a cold lobster and a bottle. You have the fixings in your kitchenette. We just had a quiet little evening together. . . . The bottle was Mumm's. Understand?"

"Yes, Mr. Morrison."

"Hook onto those facts and they may save me a lot of trouble. I mean, suppose that the police were to drop in on you. That's what I mean. I came in last night about seven with a lobster and a bottle of Mumm's, and we just had a quiet little evening together. Just in case they ask."

For once, she looked at him without a smile.

"I'll keep the newspaper johnnies off," he said, sweating all at once.

"Yes, Mr. Morrison," she said.

"And I *am* coming over soon," declared Morrison. "That's all, Rose."

"Yes, Mr. Morrison," she said.

IT WAS TIME to stop work very shortly after this, so Rose Taylor closed her desk, put on her hat, and slipped her silk coat over her dress. She always wore a frock that rustled. She could hardly have told you why she always wore a frock that rustled. It was simply an instinct in her, no doubt, and that was why men looked up when she passed, startled by her beauty, and thought of open fields of flowers and a spring wind stirring them. She always walked home, for the exercise, with her eyes continually lowered but never lifting without that smile. To see her was to remember, suddenly, childhood, motherhood, and all sorts of thoughts too tender-footed for the sidewalks of New York.

She lived in a walk-up in the East Fifties. It was quite far east, to be sure, but she was only on the third floor and anyone who really wanted to see her could take that much trouble. It was a neat little apartment done in green and violet because Rose liked a cool effect. For the winter months she had a nice big fireplace that would hold the eye and warm the walls.

Now, as she entered, she saw in the service pantry a big basket of flowers. She stooped to love the roses first. Then she took up the card which accompanied them. Without reading it, she touched the flame of a cigarette lighter to the card. She looked out the window, smiling at the view over the East River while the flame took hold, then she dropped the card

32

into the fireplace. Afterwards she went to the telephone and dialed a number. Presently she was saying:

"Hello, Sid. . . . Big Jeff is all excited . . . as much as diamonds, in fact. . . . He was here last night, it seems. . . . Please come over, Sid, and talk about it."

She rang off, changed her frock and shoes in the dressing room, touched the brightness of her hair, and then took care of the roses. They were hardly placed before a knock came at the door and Sid Pollok entered.

"Hello, kid," he said. "What's eating the Big Boy?"

She waited with her grave eyes down until he kissed her. Then she looked up at him with her smile.

"You see?" she said, and showed the ring.

He took her to the light so that he could study the gems with a more professional care.

"I've got a mind to sock the big mug," he declared, with a pretended anger. "I thought this was as far as he'd go."

He indicated the apartment with a glance and then straightened a little into a more dignified position, because he had seen his image in a mirror. Whenever he saw his dark, handsome face, he realized that he had something to live up to.

"How much does it mean, Sid?"

"About fifteen hundred smacks is all," he answered. "All because he wants to have been here last night? Well, it's not enough, Rose."

"I don't think so, either," she said. "But I thought I'd ask you."

He sank into a chair. She put a smoking table beside it and lighted his cigarette.

"When you think what we got!" said Sid. His mind was distracted. He could still see himself in the mirror but, although he wanted to give his full attention to the business at hand, he could not find an energy cruel enough to make him change his position. "When you think what we got . . . with all of them!" said Sid Pollok. "Is that sweet or is it not sweet? Do we stop work?"

She lifted her eyes to him with her softest smile.

33

"Darling, did you ever work?" she asked.

"Lay off, will you?" said Pollok. "I've always been waiting for the right kind of an opening. That's all. You know that. I wouldn't take the first thing that came along, like any common mug. After we clean this up, Hollywood, baby."

"Yes, dear," said Rose, dreaming on the bright, running tide of the East River. It only seems to run with the wind, people say, and the same driftwood floats back and forth between the same places—driftwood and other things.

"Big Jeff is scared, is he?" said Pollok. "But it's nothing the way he's gonna be scared. I'm gonna throw a wow into him, kid. You know what he'll do, the big pink-faced bum?"

"What will he do, Sid?" asked the girl, still smiling at her dream.

"He'll cry, that's what he'll do. He'll have to write three checks instead of one, the first two will be all spoiled with tears. What do you think we could pull him down for?"

"I don't know, Sid. I really don't know. In round numbers, do you think a hundred thousand dollars?"

"Hey, wait a minute, wait a minute. Don't be so damned round as all that. That's getting the wish out of the bone. Wait a minute. Fifty grand, I'd say. The big fat welsher, if we put him under the gun, we ought to get fifty thousand out of him before he'll let me tell the cops that he was out at Barry's house last night."

"With a gun, Sid," said the girl.

"Would I forget that? I would not. But you've got the old bean that always works. Where did you get that bean, Rose?"

"I don't know," she said.

"You wouldn't," said Pollok, "but that's all right. . . . When I think it was your steer that made us follow him last night!"

"And I suggested that we stay on a while after he left," said Rose, softly.

"Yeah, and would we have missed the biggest fish of all if we hadn't stayed?"

"You mean Willett?" asked the girl. "Don't you think he might stick in the throat just a little, Sid?"

34

"You think he's too tough for me?" asked Pollok. "What do I always tell you? The bigger they are the harder they fall."

"They make a bigger target, I suppose," she said. "But I really wouldn't."

"You wouldn't what?"

"I wouldn't bother Richard Willett."

"Why wouldn't you?"

"I just wouldn't."

"Old instinct working?"

"Yes. Right in my throat. I wouldn't trouble Richard Willett."

"And let him come off clean? Listen, baby, we'd only be reasonable. He gets a hundred thousand berries out of the will. Well, we can make a clean split with him. Fifty–fifty."

"I really wouldn't bother him," said the girl.

"Quit it, Rose. You boil me all up when you talk like that. If you keep it up, I'm going to go and have a man-to-man with him."

She shook her head. "No, you won't do that," she said.

"You think he's got the sign on me?" said Pollok. He grew so excited that for a moment he forgot his image in the mirror.

"Darling, you won't have a man-to-man with *him*," said Rose. "But there's Jacqueline Barry, you know. You might have a man-to-man with her."

"She's going to be our pet," declared Pollok. "All the rest are the small-time stuff but she's an annuity, 's what I mean."

"I wonder," mused Rose.

"Don't wonder. It's a fact. Just take it the most reasonable way. Five million smacks is what she gets. The damned death duties take half of that along with income tax. Say she don't raise more'n four percent. That's a hundred thousand kicks a year. Do we come down on her now like another death duty just because she paid a visit to Barry yesterday evening? No, Rose. No, baby. We just cut ourselves in for ten percent. . . . Look, Rose. That's using the bean, isn't it? We only declare ourselves in for ten thousand cracks a year."

"It seems that way, darling, doesn't it?" murmured Rose.

35

"When I first laid an eye on you, I said you were my luck," said Pollok, "and I was right? Baby, was I right! The thing is for you to go to Jacqueline and lay the cards right on the table."

"Oh, but Sid. I shouldn't appear except in a pinch."

"Why not? How would I get to her? But you could smile your way through any door in New York. You go and see her and lay the cards face up before her."

"Well . . . ," she said. "You know, Sid, there's another thing. What did you do when you went into the house last night?"

He slithered out of his chair and leaned over her.

"What in hell you mean?" he demanded.

"You *are* a silly darling. What else *should* I mean?" said Rose, and kept smiling at her dream of the East River.

7

❖

"A Gun and $1000"

W illett lay on the couch in his room with a map pasted
on a huge cardboard braced against his lifted knee. The
contours of the survey lines he hardly heeded, the district was
so familiar to him. He had looked at that map for thirty days,
hours at a time, always figuring out a plan of attack that could
not be developed. Perhaps that was because his instinct was to
deliver on every problem a crushing frontal attack, one of those
Napoleonic cleaver strokes at the center.

Now, because his mind was dust and ashes from long brooding on the problem, it retreated from the direct line and his eye
wandered over the back country. That was how he came to the
idea. Behind the mine the slope continued toward the east for
a mile, there running down into the white cactus valley where
a jackrabbit could not find enough fodder to sustain life in a
square league of the country, not even a Nevada rabbit used to
a half mile of loping between bites.

The valley wound around into the alkali flat—and here was
the beauty of the thing. He would not have remembered this
but the contour lines showed it perfectly. There was a continually dropping slope from east to west all across the flats—all the
way to the smelter beyond the trough of the creek bed!

He lay back and laughed. That was what New York did to a
man, now and then. Like a good drink it knocked the dead day
out of the brain and cleared the way for new ideas. The track
would have to be four times as long as he had been trying to
plan it, but once it was built, the ore from the mine was as good
as delivered at the door of the smelter. It was such low-grade

stuff that haulage costs would cut the throat of every profit, but on the longer track, with no attempt to cut through the sharp hills that lay directly between the mines and the smelter, gravity would do the entire trick. The loaded cars running down would pull the empties back—and so the thing was done.

Old Mac, out there, had been frying beans in bacon fat for twenty years and trying to find a miraculous solution. Old Mac, when he was cut in on half the profits after the track was built and the cars bought, would think that God had intervened.

Willett dropped the map and picked his whiskey and soda off the table. He sat up and raised it with a ceremonious gesture as though to some other presence in the room before he drank.

Here there was a ring at the door.

"Come in!" he called out.

A big, squat, wide-shouldered man came in. His left hand was crushing his hat.

"If I telephoned up, I knew you wouldn't see me. So I sneaked," he said. "You remember me, Mr. Willett?"

Willett eyed him in silence. The big fellow walked farther into the light and stood, well-braced.

"You're the one who quit to Benny Marley, a few years back," said Willett. "You're Slogger Haines."

"That's right," said the Slogger.

"Then get out," said Willett.

The Slogger drew back a step and paused. Willett stood up. "Get out," he said.

"If I get out, I go to hell," said the Slogger.

"That's where double-crossing rats all go," answered Willett. "I backed you, and you quit like a dog. I saw you take that sock in the mouth. Get out of my sight!"

The Slogger turned and went slowly to the door. He had it open when Willett said, "All right! All right! Come back here!"

The Slogger turned back and shut the door. His eyes avoided Willett.

"That dirty scrap finished you, didn't it?" asked Willett.

"Yes, sir," said the Slogger.

"What do you want from me? Twenty dollars? All right, here it is."

The Slogger looked at the money and shook his head.

"The kid's flat," he said.

"Who's the kid?"

"Marie Le Beau."

"Vaudeville?"

"Burlesque, Mr. Willett."

"What's knocked her flat?"

"I dunno. One of them things in the hospital. The kid's flat."

"She's a crooked little four-flusher, isn't she?"

"Well . . . she's not little, Mr. Willett."

"One of the big, quantity-production, sugar-cured hams?"

"Yes, sir."

"Was she ever straight with you?"

"No, sir."

"Why don't you let her go?"

"She's got no place to go, sir."

"Ah, hell!" said Willett.

He went back to his drink and took a good swallow of it.

"Open the top drawer of the dresser," he directed.

The Slogger obeyed.

"What's in there?"

"A wallet and a big rod," said the Slogger, with a certain new emotion.

"Put the gun in your pocket and see what's in the wallet."

"After a moment: "Eleven hundred and fifteen dollars, sir."

"Leave a hundred and fifteen inside," said Willett.

"My God, sir . . ."

"Shut up, Slogger. It's poker money and doesn't count. . . . Good-bye."

"Mr. Willett. . . ."

"Quit that, will you?"

"Yes, sir. But I wish. . . ."

"Feed it to her by the week. . . . How old are you?"

"Twenty-eight, sir."

"Could you get in shape again?"

"They'd never take me on again. They know I've been a dog. They wouldn't take me on."

"They will, though," said Willett. "Go down to the Garden tomorrow and see Ralph Tozer. Tell him I sent you. If he shows you the gate, tell him again that I sent you. He'll know what I mean. Now go on home."

"If I ever get inside the ropes again. . . ."

"Quit it," said Willett. "I hate to see how they've softened you up."

He took the big hand. He could feel the ridge of the broken metacarpal bones.

"When you get in there," said Willett, "they're going to ride you and wait for you to wilt. They don't know that it was only money you fell for. You're going to knock a row of these dubs kicking. Good-bye, Slogger."

When he turned away from the door he walked up and down the room for a moment. Then he took another drink. He clenched his fist and looked at the smooth back of it. He rubbed the hard straight bones under the brown skin.

The telephone rang.

"Hello, Richard," said Jacqueline Barry. "Do you ever take tea?"

"It breaks me all up if I miss the old Ceylon," said Willett.

"It's six o'clock, so I suppose you couldn't take another drop?"

"Say where," said Willett.

"In the small dining room at the Plaza."

"I'll be over in five minutes."

He was there on time. She had a corner table with two silver covers on it and silver pitchers. She was wearing a reddish-brown tweed with a green scarf. Her hat was just right on her red hair.

"In fact, it's so late that I'll have to have a Scotch," said Willett.

"I was afraid that might be so," she said, and raised her hand

40

to signal the waiter. Her handkerchief drifted toward the floor and he caught it. She tucked it away again as he gave his order. A small, clean fragrance stayed in the air.

"The other day, Richard," she said, "when you said you wanted to see a bit more of me . . . well, I need to see you now. Does it make a lot of difference to you if I'm in some stupid trouble?"

"For good and for evil," said Willett, "and all that sort of thing. Go on."

She did not go on. She buttered a section of toast, looked at it, ate it, forgot him with her eyes for a moment. He sipped his Scotch.

"What are you thinking of, Richard?" she asked.

"I was thinking that women have mouths like babies, sometimes. I mean, they stay childish a long time."

"That's because my teeth were wrong," she said. "I'm not a baby, Richard. Sometimes people are fooled."

"I'm not fooled," said Willett.

"People come to you when they're in trouble," she stated.

"A lot of people get trouble when they come to me," he replied.

"I wonder how strictly honest you are," said Jacqueline.

"Do you?"

"Shall I be polite? Do I have to be the winning girl?" she asked.

"Just be natural," said Willett.

"Man-to-man, are you an honest man, Richard?"

"Man-to-man . . . yes, sometimes."

"I mean, always straight?"

"No."

"Not always?"

"Not by a damned sight."

"You're being honest now."

"Whether I'm honest or not, you're going to tell me the story," he said. "Why fence?"

"That's true. Well, a very pretty, charming girl is trying to blackmail me."

41

"About a man?"

"In a way, yes. I wondered if you'd see her and try to find out something about her. If she's ready to blackmail, she must have some bad spots in her life. There ought to be some way to shut her up."

"Who is she?"

"You *will* help?"

"I asked for the story, didn't I?"

"Yes. Well, here's her name and address."

"I'll see Rose," he said.

"Thank you, Richard."

"What's the story she'll tell?"

"I don't want you to know. If you were just to say that you're representing me, and that I'm trying to raise some money, you see."

"But I ought to know what's up her sleeve. Seen in a compromising situation anywhere?"

"Not exactly. I don't want to talk."

"It isn't a love business, then. Murder, perhaps?"

"Do you think that I'd commit a murder, Richard?"

He looked into the green of her eyes for a long time. Neither of them smiled.

"Yes, I think you might," he said. "Particularly if there were five million dollars in it."

She said nothing. Her color did not change. Her eyes were perfectly steady.

"The police don't see everything," said Willett. "The other day they overlooked a handkerchief on a living room floor."

He took the bit of linen from his pocket and showed it to her. She was as steady as ever.

"What makes you think it's mine?" she asked.

"I like a woman who uses a thin perfume," said Willett.

She buttered some more toast and ate it, slowly. She knew her beauty so well that she made even the munching of toast attractive. Willett grew hungry as he watched.

"Will you give it to me?" she asked.

"No. Tell me about Telford. You love him?"

42

"Yes."

"High as the sky?"

This she considered. "Not quite," she said.

"Dead set on marrying him?"

"Yes," she said.

"You won't change your mind?"

"No."

"Well," said Willett, "here's the handkerchief, then."

8

❖

"Unpleasant Evidence"

The light that winked and died and winked forth again all
around Telford's house moved as irregularly as the flight
of a firefly. O'Rourke carried it and used it only here and
there, particularly around the old junk heap which was piled
up behind the stable. After that he circled down to the thick
brush which stood to the right of the house, toward the road-
side. Here he crouched so that the bushes themselves made a
screen between him and observation. It was patient work, and
O'Rourke was not a patient man. Now and then, snapping out
the electric torch, he cursed softly, with a tasty violence of soul.
He had a redoubled yearning for a cigar, but he could not risk
sending the scent of a cigar down the wind. The lighted windows of the house he squinted at from time to time with a
personal malevolence.

He worked down to the gutter of the road at the edge of
the bushes and flashed a ray from the lantern straight down the
slope. The ray struck what he wanted, but the tangle of wire was
far smaller than he had expected to find. He picked up the knot
of wire, squatted on his heels, and studied it at his leisure. The
soldered joinings told the trick. It was easy to stretch the
tangle roughly into the form of a lamp shade of cylindrical
shape.

He crushed it again, shoved it down into his coat pocket,
and stepped out on the road. Down it he walked with a bold
swing. As he paused to light his cigar, he thought of Campbell
and the Campbell theories about the David Barry murder.
O'Rourke had to laugh. He kept on laughing softly until he

reached the car he had parked in the side road a little farther on. It was a small car, but it could do eighty miles an hour or more. O'Rourke, on this night, did not use all that speed. He let the machine drift at thirty-five and leaned back against the cushion with the almost sleepy indifference of a contented man.

IT WAS SOME TIME before this that Willett, in his room at the hotel, walked up and down before his windows watching the lowering of the sun in the west and mapping in his mind a form of campaign. The jangle of the telephone was repeated several times before it reached the attention of Willett.

The voice of the Slogger came over the wire.

"I've seen your friend at the Garden!" he said. "I couldn't wait . . . I dashed up and gave the kid a handout . . . and then I jumped down to the Garden. He wouldn't hardly let me talk until I used your name. That put the grease under him. He sat down with a bump. He's gunna give me a chance to train for a month and then have a fight. What I owe you, Mr. Willett . . . ?"

"Listen," said Willett. "If you owe me something, what are you willing to do to pay it back?"

"Anything," said the Slogger.

"I'll be leaving in five minutes. Meet me on the next corner north and I'll tell you what I want."

"I'll be there," said the Slogger. "I hope you'll let me in on any trouble, Mr. Willett."

"There'll be no trouble," he said.

He hung up the phone and reached for his hat. His plan was completely organized.

DETECTIVE SERGEANT ANGUS CAMPBELL believed that backgrounds did not matter and that people were what counted, but the living room of Jacqueline Barry's house in the country disturbed him more than a little. He did not mind the eighteenth-century French furniture; it looked a bit groggy like a

45

frail, outworn aristocracy; but the wallpaper disturbed him seriously. It was one of those landscape affairs, glazed to the quality of an oil painting, and over the fireplace it displayed a lake scene with white sheep standing beside their images in the water and a reclining lady listened to a gentleman with a white wig and a guitar. It was the people in the picture that troubled Campbell. They seemed to be listening and intruding themselves so that it was hard for him to give the proper concentration to Jacqueline Barry.

She was not cordial. She was merely enduring.

"It's one of those forms that we've got to go through," he said to her.

"I suppose so," answered Jacqueline, and waited.

"I'll even have to ask what sort of a dress you had on the other evening when you went to the moving picture," said Campbell.

She got up and crossed the room to a bell. By the time she had returned to her chair a butler appeared.

"Tell Alice to bring the dress I wore the other evening. The yellow one," she said. "And the hat and shoes, please. Also the wrap."

"Thanks," said Campbell. "Then you went over to Waterton and saw a movie? What was it?"

"*The First Smile.*"

"Good one?" he asked.

"A silly thing. I couldn't sit through it."

"Who played the leads, you remember?"

"Sue Maryland and Larry Lloyd."

"You like him?"

"He's one of those sleek young Hollywood things," said the girl.

She was in riding togs and there was mud on her boots and fresh air had reddened her cheeks and dimmed her eyes a little. Campbell looked at her wrist. It was round and strong; not very big, but strong. She had good-sized hands, too. Campbell thought that the taste of people in women had gone to pot. In his mind the ideal picture was of a slim delicacy. This girl had

46

half the qualities of a boy about her. She had dashed out from town at the end of the day and flung herself into riding clothes for a two- or three-mile dash across country. That was how he understood it, as he waited to see her.

"I know," said Campbell. "Kind of a female sort of a man. I like a type like Tucker Dean more than that. You know Tucker Dean?"

"I've seen him a few times. I'm not interested in the pictures," she said.

"Not seen him lately?" asked Campbell.

"No."

He glanced down at the floor for a moment, and looked up to find that a maid had entered the room carrying the outfit for which the girl had sent. He gave it one glance.

"Hold it up for Mr. Campbell, the dress and then the wrap," said the girl.

The maid obeyed. As for Campbell, the glance had been enough, but now he used his eyes carefully merely because of practiced habit. That was why he saw, close to the hem of the skirt, a small green splotch. A grass stain, perhaps.

"Thanks," said Campbell. "That's all."

"Thank you, Alice," said the girl.

The maid went out, smiling, as though she had performed some notable action.

"You see," said Campbell, "when it's a case like this, a lot of money, we have to make long reports. You know, maybe."

"I suppose so," said Jacqueline. "What did all that about color-blindness mean?"

"Nothing," said Campbell. "Just running down everything." He paused and then added, quietly, "They tied me to O'Rourke. I can't help all the funny ideas that an O'Rourke gets. Irishmen shoot quick, but they keep on missing."

The last remark warmed his blood a bit. When he was out in his car again, he compressed his lips and then stretched them at the corners. He was not altogether pleased with this interview for reasons that he would give to O'Rourke later on. In the meantime, through the twilight, he was speeding back to New

47

York. It was quite dark when he pulled up near Pêche d'Or, and went into the place.

Some of the staff had been held over from the old speakeasy days and therefore Campbell received quick and obsequious attention. The proprietor came with a smiling face and fear in his eyes.

"Ever see Richard Willett in here?" asked Campbell. "Big brown-faced man, six-feet-two and something, a hundred and ninety pounds, looks hard and fit. Mostly hard."

"I don't place him, Sergeant," said the proprietor. "Sit down and have a drink?"

"Here's a picture of him," said Campbell. "Show it around to your waiters and barmen without saying why."

The little fat man came back through the jangle and roar of the crowd with a barman in tow. The barman might not have been "told," but he looked frightened. His sallow face was finely beaded with sweat from the haste of his work during this rush hour.

"This is Sammy; he saw your man," was the introduction. "Sammy, meet Sergeant. . . ."

"All right," said Campbell. "You saw this fellow in here?"

"Yes," said Sammy. "Yes, sir."

"Last night?"

"Yes, sir."

"The night before?"

"Yes, sir."

"The night before, eh?"

"Yes, sir. Last night he asked for the same thing he'd had the night before."

"Humph," said Campbell. "What time was he in here . . . the night before, I mean."

"The same both nights. Around nine-thirty."

"That's all," said Campbell, and turned on his heel and stalked out.

When evidence did not turn up the way he wanted it to, he hated the world. That was why he had few happy moments in his life.

On the curb, he stood for a moment, pulling out his upper lip and letting it flick back against his teeth, while he rolled his bald eyes at the street lights. He was seeing the face of O'Rourke, with the fat sneer of contentment on it.

And still, Campbell swore to himself that he would prove that Telford was not the guilty man. Willett—Willett was the murderer to the taste of Sergeant Campbell. He got into his car and drove down to headquarters.

9

❖

"Murder by Wire"

The sun was dropping, that evening, when Willett got to the door of the apartment of Rose Taylor.

"I'm representing Miss Barry," he said.

She looked up to him with her smile and said, "Oh!" and drew back to let him enter.

"If you sit down here," said Rose, "you can see the sunset colors on the East River. They flow around on the water just like oils. Have you ever noticed?"

"Have you got anything to drink, Rose?" asked Willett.

She hesitated only a moment.

"Of course I have," she said, with her smile. "What sort of a cocktail do you . . . ?"

"Whiskey," said Willett, "and never mind any fixings."

She paused to look back at him, graceful in her pausing; then she went on. She was gone some time. It seemed to Willett that he heard a slight metallic clicking and a murmuring voice, as though someone were speaking over a telephone. He walked back to the end of the room away from the river and, looking out, he saw by the sunset light the huge bulk of the Slogger loitering on the opposite pavement.

Willett sauntered back and stood at gaze, the river before him, splendor running on its face. He turned when Rose came back, carrying a tray.

"I'm sorry I was so long," said Rose. "The ice tray stuck in the Frigidaire and I couldn't budge it. I thought of calling for you. You could have done it in an instant, of course. . . . Is this the sort of whiskey you like? I never can tell."

She had a bottle of bourbon, old, and another of Scotch. He picked up the Scotch and looked at it with care.

"Where did you get this stuff?" he asked.

"Oh, that was sent to me by a friend for Christmas."

"What a friend that was," said Willett, and poured a stiff three fingers. "Do you know my name?"

"I ought to, shouldn't I? I'm sure that I've seen you somewhere. But then you come from Miss Barry and I'm glad to see you. She *is* lovely, isn't she?"

This enthusiasm made Rose Taylor glow like the sunset on the East River. Willett did not hurry to answer. He sat down and enjoyed the picture of the girl, smiling a little.

"What about a drink?" he asked.

"I don't drink, really," said Rose, "unless someone feels uncomfortable about drinking alone. Does it make you feel odd to drink alone?"

"Have a shot," said Willett. "It will do you good. Steady the nerves, and all that."

"Shall I?" she said. "Well. . . ."

She poured a small measure and squirted seltzer into it. Not too much seltzer, either.

"Here's mud in your eye," said Willett.

"Your good health," said the girl, shining her eyes at him over the edge of her glass.

They drank. "The seltzer puts tingles in the eyes, doesn't it?" she said, wiping hers with a delicate fluff of handkerchief.

"My name is Willett," he told her.

"I'm so glad to know you, Mr. Willett."

"Listen, Rose. Are you going to play it all the way to the finish like this? Baby-blue eyes, and all that?"

At this, she looked down to the floor, gravely, shrinking a little.

"While we're talking," he said, "if one of the boy friends should drop in, it would be a mistake."

"If someone should drop in?" she repeated, blankly.

"It would be a hell of a mistake. It would make a mess all over the place," said Willett. "Come here, Rose."

51

He went to the rear window of the long room and pointed. "You see the big boy across the street?" he asked.

"Yes," she answered.

"Shall I send him away?"

She looked up at him without her smile. Then she shrugged her shoulders and laughed. "All right, you send him away," she said.

He stared at her for another moment, then lifted the window and leaned on the sill. He made a gesture. The Slogger turned on his heel and went off.

"If you'll excuse me, I ought to telephone right away. I forgot something," said Rose Taylor.

"I thought you had," answered Willett.

He went back to the front window to watch the sliding and dimming colors of the East River. A tug was butting against the tide under the vast arch of the bridge. In another room a voice murmured, the telephone clicked softly. Rose came back.

"Now we can sit down and talk," said Willett.

She slipped into a chair and laughed a little.

"Won't it rest you?" he asked.

"Of course it will."

"What sort of a front do you walk behind on weekdays?"

"Front, Mr. Willett? Oh!"

"You can't step off the stage, Rose, can you?"

"I'm trying to," said Rose.

"How long ago did you take this part?"

"I was about fifteen," she said.

"At it ever since?"

"Yes, I suppose so."

"Tell me what you're supposed to do during the week?"

"I'm the secretary of Mr. Jeffrey Morrison."

"Oh, secretary? How is he to work for?"

"He's very kind."

"I'll bet he is. He looks so kind that I'm surprised that you had to bother about Jacqueline Barry."

She interlaced her fingers and could not answer until she had pulled them apart again.

"Don't you think it's better to have two strings to one's bow?" she asked.

"Use some more of that whiskey," said Willett. "It may change you unawares."

"Yes, Mr. Willett," she said, and took another drink. He followed his own command and waited for the smoke in his brain, the fire in his stomach, the sour in his throat.

"You're a hard little devil, Rose," he said.

"Yes, Mr. Willett," she said.

"About Jacqueline Barry . . . how much do you want?"

"Well, it was foolish of Jacqueline Barry, don't you think? To go there through the storm, so late at night and all? I mean, since she was to inherit all those millions?"

"You think she bumped off Barry?"

"I just wondered a little."

"You think any girl would have been able to strangle Barry and then tie him to the balcony railing like a sausage put up to cure in the air? Do you think she could do that?"

"Yes, don't you, Mr. Willett?"

"Rose, do you want some good advice?"

"I love good advice. I'd love to have some from you."

"Haul out of this."

"I don't think that I could do that," she said.

"Come over here, will you? Sit down on the arm of my chair. That's better. Now I can see you, tricks and all. You're really lovely. Anything as smooth as you could be washed clean pretty easily. Why don't you wash the dirt out of your rotten little soul?"

"Yes, Mr. Willett."

"Ah, quit it, will you?"

"I want to quit it. I want to talk your way. It's the way I like, but I've kept up the song and dance so long I'd feel naked and exposed if I threw away the props. I don't *know* what I am inside."

"Tears, eh?" said Willett. "Well, that's a surprise."

"You're making a frightful fool of me."

"No, I'm trying to be fatherly, damn it. Go back to your own chair."

She went back to her own chair.

"How much did you expect to grab from Jacqueline Barry?" he asked.

"She's going to be so frightfully rich. . . . I think I'll go wash my face."

"Don't do it. How much from Miss Barry?"

"I thought she could easily spend a few thousand a year."

"Annuity, eh?"

"It seems an awfully safe sort of a thing to have."

"Who put the idea into your head?"

"It was . . . I thought of it myself."

"Who put the idea into your head?"

"Sid thought . . . oh!"

"Sid who?"

"Please stop," said Rose.

"Well, all right," said Willett. "But this blackmail business is the bunk. You couldn't keep it up. It would burn you before long."

She was silent.

"You're going to drop it from now on."

"I can't," she said.

"Sid won't let you?"

She was silent again.

"Do you know what a beautiful bit of hell could be started around this?"

"Yes," she said. "I don't know what to do!"

The telephone rang.

"Maybe that will tell you," said Willett, as she started up. "Shall I go to the phone with you?"

"No," she said.

"Shall I go to the phone with you?"

"Please do," said Rose.

He went with her into the bedroom. It was all cushioned with silk. It was a blue and golden room, like Rose. The telephone was white lacquer with an inlaid pattern of Siamese silver work.

"Yes?" said Rose into the phone. "Yes, Sid. . . ."

She looked up with a guilty start toward Willett.

Then she was saying: "No, it's all right . . . I mean just that. . . . It's all right. . . . It would take explaining. What's happening with you . . . ? Have you . . . ? Yes, he's here. . . . Yes, I could call him. Shall I . . . ?

The sound that came over the wire now might have been caused by the clapping of two hands together, close to the mouthpiece at the other end of the line. But there was a more lasting resonance to the explosion.

The girl screamed, "Sid! Sid!"

For answer, there was the cold little click of a receiver being hung up.

"They've murdered him!" whispered Rose.

"Let him go," said Willett. "The dirty rat was eating your heart, if you have a heart. He was eating your heart, wasn't he, Rose?"

"Yes," she said.

"Come back into the other room. That's right. You're as steady as a clock. Sit down here and look at your East River. There's still some of your color in it. Take this drink. Clink glasses with me. You don't want to get in the same sort of hell that Sid is in, do you? I'm telling you that because I know all about hell. . . . I'm drinking to you, Rose. Do you feel better now?"

"Yes," she said.

"When the police find him, will they be able to tie him to you? Will they be able to tie you into this?"

"I don't know. I don't think so."

"What will you do this evening?"

"I'm going somewhere."

"Of course you are. You're going to bed."

"Yes," she said.

"Good night, Rose."

55

She went with him as far as the door and paused there, leaning her forehead against his shoulder.

"I know," said Willett, "but you'll be brand new in the morning. Keep your eyes clear and you'll be able to walk the line. Good night."

10

❖

"O'Rourke *versus* Campbell"

Sid Pollok had been in the highest spirits. A bubbling gaiety such as he rarely enjoyed kept fountaining up from his soul into his throat. He could not sit still in his chair but had to jump up now and then and walk his room. It was decorated in part with pictures of pretty girls, but the chief decoration was a series of pictures of Sid Pollok. They were arranged side by side across the expanse of one blank wall. They showed Sid in a derby, in a straw hat, in a soft felt; he was in plus-fours, tennis flannels, tweeds, a dinner jacket, tails. In one, he was glorious in a morning coat, with a tall hat, gloves clasped in one hand which also held or rested on a stick, a gardenia in his button-hole, and his most charming smile was on his lips.

Sometimes Sid thought of sending the whole caboodle of pictures right out to Hollywood to knock the dummies out of their chairs. Sometimes he thought of sending only the master-piece of the morning coat. But he hesitated. It was an impor-tant move and advices differed. The majority said that the best thing was to wait until the Hollywood nuts heard about him and invited him in. That was the way to get the big dough right from the start; otherwise you go out there and sit around and nothing happens except that you get knifed in the back. But on the other hand, if you wait to be invited, who knows? People are so dumb. There's a lot of jealousy, too. The people that have eyes, they carry a knife up the sleeve. The poor clucks that haven't any eyes, they don't count, anyway. Sometimes, Sid Pollok was on the verge of simply taking his pictures and spreading himself for some new rags, and going right out there to Hollywood where somebody could see him. Otherwise, some lily like Larry Lloyd would go on breaking the hearts and collecting the smacks by the thousand. Larry Lloyd got eight thousand a week, somebody said. Think of it, a cluck like Larry Lloyd. What had he got? Nothing!

Here Mr. Pollok answered a knock at his door, and let in a visitor. Mr. Pollok opened the door with his left hand and kept his right hand on the snub-nosed automatic in his coat pocket.

"Hello," said Pollok, as he closed the door. "How's things? Glad to see you—all I *can* see of you. With that coat collar up and that hat pulled down you look like mumps, or something. . . . Excuse me, but it's just my way to sort of run on. . . . No? Have a drink? No? Well, suppose we get down to business then. I've thought it over. No bleeding. I know what you get out of this. I know just where you stand, so we're out in the clear. Would it look good for you to be spilled to the newspapers, all about that visit at night to the house of Dave Barry? What did the medical examiner say? Bumped off about ten o'clock? You know, it wouldn't look good; so I said to myself that I wouldn't spill the stuff. I'd keep it. Maybe you and me could arrange something. So I thought, about twenty-five thousand smacks would be all. I know what it means to you, this deal, but I thought I'd be reasonable. Twenty-five thousand smacks is all, I said to myself. So how about it?"

"Suppose we talk," said the visitor.

"Sorry. I got a date. You come across or put the old name on the dotted line. Otherwise, I have to grab the phone like this, and dial a number. Shall I go on dialing?"

The visitor said nothing.

"Well, I told you I had a date," said Pollok, "so here goes to spill the soup. . . . Hello! Hello! Is that you . . . Anything going wrong . . . ? What do you mean it's going all right? All right for you and me. . . ? Well, I've got him here. . . . I want to speak to your friend. Is he there . . . ? Can you call him to the phone? I've got a story that ought to break big. . . ."

Pollok had been keeping an eye on his visitor, up to this moment, but now the warmth of ideas made him look only toward the telephone. It was then that the visitor drew the automatic from his pocket. It came out with a gliding movement. He fired once.

Pollok turned abruptly toward the wall. He began to slide down in his chair. It would not be necessary for the visitor to shoot again. He hung up the telephone and watched Pollok sliding down and down. His dead body eased itself smoothly and limply toward the floor. At the last moment it went more quickly. The head struck with a bump. It turned to the side, covering against the rug the hole the bullet had made in entering. Pollok was smiling with his eyes half-open. He had an arm stretched out as though offering to shake hands.

The visitor leaned down and opened Pollok's coat and pushed something into the inner pocket. Then he stood up and looked himself over with care. Footfalls were beginning to trample on the floor above. The visitor went out into the hall.

"I thought I heard something," said a woman's voice, coming down the stairs from the floor above. "Maybe it was a door slamming, but it sounded to me like a gun in Mr. Pollok's room."

"We'll go look and see," said a man.

The visitor smiled, then he went down the lower stairs without haste. When he reached the sidewalk, he dusted his gloved hands together, and then he turned down the street. Two corners away, he took off his overcoat. The night was much too warm for that.

SERGEANT O'ROURKE had a desk in the corner of the big room. There was no reason why he should have the commanding privacy of a desk in the corner. Sergeant Angus Campbell was of an equal seniority and his services had been so superior that only Sergeant Campbell knew the extent of that superiority. But O'Rourke was a grafter. That was the truth about it. O'Rourke could send his family to the country in the summer, and how are you going to do that and live on Lexington Avenue the rest of the year? How, on a sergeant's salary? Don't be funny! Sergeant Campbell's desk was away out in the middle of the room, lost among the commoners.

Well, one day the papers would get O'Rourke. Newspapers are stupid and they're dirty, but eventually they get the crooks and pillory them. O'Rourke would commit suicide or something. Campbell would write a nice letter to the widow.

He considered these thoughts as he stared across the room toward the Irishman that night. O'Rourke was smoking one of his thick cigars and resting his heels on the edge of his desk. Not on the varnish. Heel scars on the varnish of a desk made the inspector sour. He always kept a blotter firmly fixed and right up to the edge of the desk.

Anger gradually worked lower and lower in the throat of Angus Campbell. When he was able to speak, and be sure that his voice would be under safe control, he went across to the Irishman.

"Hello, Angus," said O'Rourke. "You been in long? I was waiting to see you."

"Yeah, you were, were you?" said Campbell.

"I wanted to find out how the case was going," said O'Rourke.

"What've you been doing?" asked Campbell, glowering.

"Oh, I been around. The inspector manages to keep me busy, one way or another."

"You're one of these three-days-a-week men, eh?" said the Scotchman. "You work Monday, Wednesday, and Friday, eh?"

"I'm not a credit to the force like you are," said O'Rourke. "The only thing is, the guys higher up, they don't know how I take it easy. You wouldn't tell 'em, would you, Angus? An old pal like you wouldn't tell them, would he?"

"Ah-h-h-h!" said Campbell. He swallowed. Then he was able to speak again.

"What about Willett? When does he go to the chair?" asked O'Rourke.

"Did you check up on his alibi?" asked Campbell.

"I didn't have to. I knew you would," said O'Rourke. "I

suppose that alibi was all rotten? Nobody ever seen him at La Pêche d'Or?"

Campbell said, "What about the girl?"

"Matilda? Oh, did Matilda Grunsky do it?" asked O'Rourke, eagerly.

Campbell lighted a cigarette. He was breathing so hard that his breath knocked out the flame of the match the first time.

"Jacqueline Barry . . . ," said Campbell.

"It's her, is it?" said O'Rourke. "I wouldn't have thought that, Angus. Big enough, strong enough, cool enough to do it, all right. But I wouldn't have thought she was the one."

"Jacqueline Barry," said Campbell, looking O'Rourke straight in the eye, "didn't go to Waterton, didn't see *The First Smile*. She didn't even know that Tucker Dean was in the cast of the picture. All she knew was what a newspaper heads up an ad with. She never saw *The First Smile*. She was lying about where she was that night."

"Was she?" said O'Rourke. "Has she gotta burn for it? If she wasn't at Waterton, she must of been at the Barry house, I guess. Nothing else she would of lied about. I mean, take a girl like that, she wouldn't have a date that she wanted to keep secret, would she? No, I guess she must of been the one that killed Barry. We'll arrest her and let the jury send her to the electric chair, then, because she didn't see *The First Smile*. We'll have the laugh on Jacqueline Barry then, all right."

Campbell said: "I've told you something. What do *you* tell?"

"I was just playing around," said O'Rourke, yawning. "All I found was this. Maybe one of your kids would like to play with it. They don't have many toys."

He tossed a little knot of wire onto the desk top and closed his eyes as he puffed smoke toward the ceiling.

Campbell began to examine the tangle of wire. A young detective came in, slumped at his desk, began to write a report.

"What was it, Jerry?" asked someone.

"Petty larceny mug bumped off in the East Fifties . . . the Far East Fifties," said Jerry. "Got a little record behind him . . . little petty larceny record, is all."

"Where?" asked Campbell of O'Rourke, holding up the wire. "Where'd you get it?"

"Where? Oh, I found it on the place of a friend of yours. Out in the bushes. Just happened to pick it up because I thought one of your kids might like to play with it. Telford's the name of the place where I found it."

Campbell stood up.

"It could have been planted!" he said.

"Sure it could," agreed O'Rourke, blandly. "Sure it could have been planted. All the way through, everything could have been planted. Maybe God planted it, the same as He made Telford color-blind."

Campbell sat down slowly. He kept the wire tangle in his hands. He started to speak; stopped.

Jerry was saying, "One of those mugs that the girls fall for. Look what I brought away to hang in my room and keep me company. Is this a looker? Not very long in from the country. Her name is Rose. Wrote out on the back. Rose Taylor. 'Fairer than the lily and brighter than the rose. . . .' Not brighter than this Rose, though."

Campbell stood up and went to Jerry's desk.

"You loot the rooms of dead men, eh?" he asked. "Give me that picture."

"Yes, sergeant," said Jerry, jumping to his feet. "I only wanted to say that. . . ."

"Shut up," said the sergeant. "You got the making of a sneak thief, not a detective. . . . What's the name of this yegg that's been knocked over?"

"Sidney K. Pollok," said Jerry.

"Address?"

"Here you are, sir."

"I've got a mind to turn you in for this bit of work," said the sergeant. "A couple more bits like this and you go out where there's more fresh air."

The sergeant turned on his heel and left the room.

He went straight down to the street, got in his car, and shot it rapidly uptown. When he pulled up to the curb, at last, where the sour smell of the East River was in the air, another car stopped just behind him and the bulk of O'Rourke bundled itself out after him.

"You had a sort of a lonely look when you started out," said O'Rourke. "I wouldn't want to have you wanderin' around the big town all depressed and lonesome, Angus. So I just come along."

11

❖

"Collapsing Alibis"

A policeman guarded the door. He stood up and saluted. "Lieutenant Morrissey is coming, Sergeant," he said.

"Let him come," said O'Rourke. "Let him come, and give him my regards. Show us what's in here."

When the door was open, the policeman pointed out the facts. O'Rourke and Campbell listened.

"Medical examiner has been. Instant death from a bullet, forty-five caliber, through the head. Was sitting in that chair, and slid out of it. Looks kind of natural, don't he, lying that way?"

"That stuff on the desk out of his pockets?"

"Yes, Sergeant."

"What's your name?" asked Campbell.

"Stacey, sir."

"Stacey, back up and close the door." The door closed.

"Morrison spent the evening with a Rose Taylor," said O'Rourke. "I see how you figure it, Angus. Morrison was Barry's partner, and if he spent the evening with Rose, and Rose knew a fellow by the name of Pollok, and Pollok gets bumped off, then either Rose or Pollok is guilty as hell and oughta burn for it. Rose, most likely. See how it works out? Pollok strangles Barry in bed. Rose makes up the bed afterwards to plant the thing so's it looks like suicide. Look at all those female touches about the making of the bed, and all. It's as straight as a shot. Rose and Pollok do the job. Why? Because Morrison was sore at Barry and one day he says to Rose, his secretary: 'Rose, I'm sour at that partner of mine. I'm sour at

64

Barry.' She says: 'Yes, sir. I'll give orders right away.' So she picks up her boyfriend, here, and they go out and bump off Barry. That's all clear and simple. And afterwards, they. . . ."

"Ah, God!" said Campbell. "Be still with your dirty Irish tongue, will you?"

"Mr. Campbell," said O'Rourke. "I'm dead sorry I've offended you, sir. I was just trying to do some deducing, the same as you and the book detectives do. I was tryin' to improve the old bean, the same as you're always doing."

"There's over five hundred dollars in this wallet," said Campbell.

"That's why the mug on the floor looks so happy," said O'Rourke.

Campbell gave him a look, said: "And there's a golden 'B' stamped on the cover of the wallet."

"There's a what?"

" 'B' stamped in gold," said Campbell, slowly. "The initial, I suppose, 'B' for the first letter in the name Pollok, eh?"

He turned his bald, bulging eyes upon O'Rourke.

O'Rourke's face was funny.

"I told you that Pollok turned the trick," said O'Rourke.

"Bah!" said Campbell.

O'Rourke took the wallet and turned it in his hands.

"I'll be damned!" he said. "It's a 'B' all right. We'll get Matilda Grunsky to take a look at this. Wait, I'll get her on the phone."

He sat down and dialed a number.

"I'll tell you what I deduce," said O'Rourke, as he waited for an answer. "Telford did it. I found some wire under a bush and that proves he did it. But Jacqueline Barry didn't go to a show, and that proves she did it. And Morrison has got a secretary, and that proves he did it. And the secretary has got a Pollok, and that proves she did it. . . . Hello, Miss Grunsky. This is Detective O'Rourke. . . . How are you, yourself? What sort of a wallet did Mr. Barry usually keep his pocket cash in? It was pigskin? Anything on it? Is that so? Thanks very much. That's all. Good night."

He hung up the receiver and turned from the telephone.

"Yeah," said O'Rourke. "Yeah. Pigskin, with a 'B' stamped on it. Now, what in hell do you know about that? 'Sweet Rosie O'Grady, she's my little Lady.' Look at her, Angus? Is she gonna tie us to something?"

AT THE SECOND RING, Rose Taylor opened the door. She had on a gray, soft dressing gown and soft gray slippers. The interval between the first and second rings she had spent on her hair, so that it was not very tousled—it was simply natural.

"Yes?" she said, peeping out, frightened.

"Sergeant Campbell," said O'Rourke. "I'm Detective Sergeant O'Rourke. We wanta have a little talk with you."

"Oh, do you? Come right in. What in the world do you want to talk to me about?"

She closed the door behind them and leaned against it, for this made her seem smaller still, childishly small in her heelless slippers with her knees bent ever so slightly. She looked up at them with parted lips.

"Well, take it easy," said O'Rourke. "Let's just sit down and talk things over a little, eh? Don't be nervous, Miss Taylor. You know, the police are like the doctor, they come to every man sooner or later."

"Will you take these chairs?" she asked. "And may I get you anything to drink . . . if you're going to stay a while?"

"Do that, will you?" said O'Rourke.

She went out.

O'Rourke smiled after her. Campbell's expression was glum.

"When you think of a big fat sow like Morrison takin' advantage of a poor kid like that," said O'Rourke.

"Yeah?" growled Campbell. "She's got a pretty Pollok, too."

Afterwards they sat over their drinks, and O'Rourke took the lead.

"The other evening when Jeffrey Morrison was here with you. . . ."

"Oh," said Rose. She blushed and kept her eyes fixed on the floor.

"He did spend the evening here?"

"Yes," said Rose.

"He spends a lot of evenings here?" said O'Rourke.

She bowed her head a little more and was silent.

"Damn!" said O'Rourke. "I mean, the big tub of pink butter, is what I mean. I mean, the damned, soggy. . . . Anyway, you know a fellow by name of Pollok?"

"Oh, yes," said Rose, brightly.

"Like him?"

"I'm sorry for him," said Rose.

"What's the matter with him you should be sorry for him?" asked O'Rourke.

"He's generally out of a job," said Rose.

"And you been the big sister?"

"I've helped him a little now and then, poor fellow!" said Rose.

"Yeah, he'd take a lot of helping," said O'Rourke. "How long you known him?"

"Just a short time."

"Is it gonna wear down on you to hear that he's no longer one of the boys?" asked O'Rourke, softly.

"He was shot through the head in his room, this evening," said Campbell.

"Ah!" cried Rose. "Ah! Ah!" She stood in front of her chair in the position to which pain had lifted her; her face was white.

"You would!" snarled O'Rourke at Campbell. "You'd kick her in the face with the news! Take it easy, Miss Taylor. He wasn't nothing to write home about. . . . Did he mean a lot to you?"

She sank back into the chair again.

"It's just the shock," said she. "He wasn't a great friend. It was just that I was sorry for him. I suppose poor, helpless Sid is better off, in a way . . . he was so . . . so. . . ."

"You got any idea who bumped him off?" asked O'Rourke, tenderly.

"I couldn't dream who it might have been!" she answered.

On the way down to the street, they were silent. On the pavement they talked a little in lowered voices.

"Poor kid!" said O'Rourke.

"Maybe she was lying all the way through," said Campbell. "When a young girl throws her virtue away, the rest of her decency usually goes with it. Maybe everything she said was crooked."

"I know," agreed O'Rourke, "but why bear down on that till we have to? The way it stands, it's a three-way break. Telford had reasons for wanting Barry dead. Then he gets the girl and he gets the money with her. We've got the color-blindness and the wire on him. That's more than a blank. Then there's a throw toward Jacqueline Barry. Where was she that night? Why did she lie? She hated Barry, too. And Willett alibis himself out of trouble."

"I was never a man to put faith in alibis," said Campbell.

"You was never a man to put faith in anything, not even in God Almighty, with Gabriel blowing his trumpet into the Scotch of your big ears and Moses busting the rock of the Ten Commandments over your head. . . . But let's get back to where we are, if we're anywhere."

"Leave Willett out for a minute, you blaspheming Irish bog-jumper," said Campbell. "Leave the girl out, too . . . for a minute. That leaves Telford and Pollok, and the murder between them. But what ties Pollok into this case? What brings him out there on that night?"

"If Telford was there, the way it seems he was, it's a funny thing that a yegg like Pollok should suddenly appear. What drew him in?"

"I told you this was gonna be a honey," said O'Rourke. "We're only starting."

12

❖

"Third Degree"

Willett said over the wire, "Hello, hello! That you? Hello, Jacqueline."

"Hello, Richard. This is nice. Let's talk. Are you comfortable?"

"Spilled into a big chair and just looking over the brim of it like a lot of champagne bubbles over the edge of the glass; on my left a map of the harbor where my ship is just coming in; on my right a hooker of Scotch just softened down to a decency by a squirt or two of siphon; on my knee . . . well, only a telephone, but a man can't ask for the world with a fence around it. How are you fixed?"

"In bed. . . ."

"No! Already?"

"I go to bed early every other night. There's only one light in the room. I have the French windows open and I can look across the valley and see the stars. You're silly to live in that town."

"I'll come right out," said Willett.

"Come out for lunch," said she.

"I'm always busy for lunch," said Willett. "Got any free evenings?"

"Of course I have. What have you been doing since I saw you last?"

"I've been talking to the prettiest girl you ever saw, with the prettiest name: Rose."

"How charming," said Jacqueline. "Did she talk well?"

"She won't talk," said Willett.

"Are you sure?"

"No, you can't be sure about that kind of a Rose. But I think she'll be still. Shall I be seeing you soon?"

"I forgot that this is long distance."

"Have you seen John, recently?"

"Yes, of course."

"How does he bear up?"

"He worries about color-blindness a little."

"What a pity," said Willett. "Shall I say good night?"

"I wish I knew how you managed things this evening."

"Just a little tact," said Willett.

"I don't believe that. I want to hear all about it."

"One of these days."

"You mean that just talking was enough?"

"The way it turned out. I was meant for the diplomatic service but I got switched onto Barry's concerns, and after I'd handled him for a while I wasn't fit for anything but breaking rocks. That's why I turned into mining."

"Is that what the *ship* is? A mine?"

"Low-grade ore. If I can get it to the smelter at the rate I figure on, it clears me about fifty cents a ton."

"Poor Richard!"

"Poor? A thousand tons a day makes five hundred bucks; a fifty split on that leaves two hundred and fifty. And there's a hundred thousand a year in anybody's pocket."

"I hope it works out that way."

"It won't," said Willett, "but it's a stake horse, anyway."

"You're spending a lot of money on this talk. Good night, Richard."

"Good night," said Willett.

When Campbell reported the next morning he had to look over a pair of jewel smugglers but could recognize neither. He found two detectives examining an automatic.

"Know anything about this make?" asked one.

Campbell took it in hand.

"It's a Kelmsford," he said.

"What's that?"

"It's a new automatic made by a firm in London. There's not much recoil. Accurate as a target pistol, they say, but it breaks down too easily. Too many springs and what not. Why? Who wants to introduce that?"

"We took it off a mug last night. Here's your buddy. Here's little Pat O'Rourke."

O'Rourke said, "Hello, Holmes . . . I mean, Campbell. . . . But whenever I see you I think of the great detective."

The other man laughed.

"What's this gun?" demanded Campbell, holding it forth.

"I never use a gun," said O'Rourke. "I leave them for the young members of the force. An O'Rourke goes in and holds 'em spellbound with his eye. It's a tricky-looking gat. Where'd you get it, boys?"

"A poor mug named Haines was spending a wad on his gal last night. He was trying to get a taste for wine and bar whiskey, was as high as he ever looked before. So we looked him over and he had nearly a thousand berries. Said somebody had given him the dough. Is that a laugh or not? He named the party, too, and seemed to think that we'd waste a nickel telephoning to find out about the present. He had this rod on him and no license, so he's getting a rest."

"Who is he?" asked Campbell.

"Haines is the name he used."

"There's only one place in town where he could get a gun like this," said Campbell. "We'll try there."

He looked up a number in the telephone book and said to the operator over the phone: "Get Thomas and McFree for me . . . Sergeant Campbell. Thomas and McFree, sporting goods. I can't find them in the book. Why in hell aren't the last books put up here where they can be. . . ."

He listened a moment.

"Got a nasty tongue, that lad down there," said Campbell. "There's too damned much indecent language on this police force." Then he was saying, "Hello, Thomas and McFree? Detective Sergeant Campbell speaking. You handle the new Kelmsford gun? How does it go? Wait a minute, here's the

71

number. . . . Yes, a black butt. . . . To whom? Spell it, then, will you? J-E-F-F-R-E-Y M-O-R-R-I. . . . All right! All right! I've got it!"

He turned from his desk.

"They've only sold one of those in the last three months and it didn't go to anybody named Haines. Ride him. He's a crook," said Campbell.

He got up. He found O'Rourke at his side.

"You double-crossing diamond-back!" said O'Rourke. "Are we working the case together or are we not?"

"What you mean?" asked Campbell, quite innocently.

"Don't you think I learned how to spell when I went to school?"

"Ah, they poured an education down your sink, did they?" asked Campbell. "Now what if you *can* spell? I'm not your teacher. I'm not going to give you a prize even if you can read and write."

"You're bright in the morning," admitted O'Rourke, "but the fact is that the gun Haines is packing belongs to our boy-friend, Jeffrey Morrison. How did a yegg get Morrison's gun? Tell me that."

Campbell cleared his throat. His bald eyes bulged out with dislike.

"Well, we'll go talk to him together," he said.

IN EVERY EMERGENCY the Slogger put the weight well forward on the balls of his feet as though he were about to close an opponent in the ring.

"Where'd you get this gun?" asked O'Rourke.

"I picked it up," said the Slogger.

"In the gutter?"

"I just run into it," said the Slogger.

"In the subway, maybe?"

"A friend slipped it to me."

"What friend?"

"I forget."

"Think we could make you remember?"

"No."

"You don't think we can?"

The Slogger closed his eyes and went white. He licked his lips.

"I guess I can take it," he said.

"D'you know what we can hand out?" demanded Campbell.

"I guess I can take it," said the Slogger, mildly.

"Why don't you come clean? We don't think you're a yegg. You're too dumb to be one. We're going to give you a break. Will you come clean?"

"Yes," said the Slogger.

"Well, who give you this rod?"

"A fellow by the name of Murphy."

"First name?"

"Jimmy."

"Where?"

"Out in Harlem."

"When?"

"The other night."

"What for?"

"He was on the run and he slipped me the rod."

"You were the good fellow and took the gun to keep his hands clean?"

"Yes," said the Slogger.

"Go to school with Harry Murphy?"

"No," said the Slogger. "I just knew him around."

"What sort of a looking fellow is Harry?"

"Smaller than me and. . . ."

"He's smaller, and he tells smaller lies. You dummy, you can call him Jimmy and switch to Harry, eh? What you think we are? Here Sloan, Patterson, Crosby . . . come here. Hold this mug tight. I'm gonna beat hell out of him. Give me that sandbag. . . . Now, you flat-faced Swede, who gave you this gun?"

In the silence they could count the hoarse breaths that the Slogger drew.

"I . . . don't . . . know!" he said.

"You hit him, Patterson," said O'Rourke. "Knock the damned head off his shoulders. You're stronger than I am."

Patterson drew back with a frightened scowl.

"Shall I sock him now, sergeant?" he asked.

"Will you talk, dummy?" demanded Campbell.

"No," said the Slogger.

"Hit him!" shouted Campbell. "No, wait a minute. Wait a minute. Haines, d'you know Big Jeff Morrison?"

The squinting eyes of the Slogger slowly opened. His head began to straighten up.

"No," said the Slogger.

"Come here, Angus," said O'Rourke.

They stepped into the corner of the room.

"The big sap is keeping his mouth shut for somebody," said the Irishman. "A game sort of mug, at that. Nobody would take it for the sake of a guy like Morrison, would they?"

"Maybe not," answered Campbell. "But we got to see."

"Look here. He gave the name of the bird he got the money from. Look it up and you'll find that the name was Morrison."

Campbell left the room.

O'Rourke went back to the prisoner and said, "We're givin' you a break for another couple of minutes. Been in the ring, mug, ain't you?"

"Yes," said the Slogger.

"Still in it?"

"No."

"Why not?"

"I quit to Benny Marley and then they made a dog of me."

"You never quit to anybody, big boy."

"I quit to Benny Marley. Then they made a dog of me for it."

"Well, damn me for that," said O'Rourke. "Who was it you said gave you the wad of money?"

"I never said no name," said the Slogger. He turned red.

"Think a bit," said O'Rourke. "You said a name, all right. Want it used?"

"My God, no!"

Campbell came back. "Even if you got the name, don't use it, Angus. The big boy don't want it used," said O'Rourke.

"Shall I give it to you in your ear?" asked Campbell. And he whispered, "Willett!"

O'Rourke turned back to the Slogger.

"Did Willett give you the money?"

"No," said the Slogger.

"You lie! He gave you the money. Did he give you the gun?"

"No," said the Slogger.

"You fool, you said last night when they pinched you that Willett gave you the money."

"I made up the name," said the Slogger. "There ain't any Willett."

"What's he done to you, kid? Hypnotized you?" asked O'-Rourke. "Why he's been had on the phone and he admits that he gave you the money and the rod."

"Does he?" said the Slogger. "Thank God! I thought I had to go all the way through for him. But he told you, did he?"

His head rolled back and he drew a breath that was a groan.

"You *would* go all the way through for him?" asked O'-Rourke.

"How far is all the way?" asked the Slogger. He began to rub his neck as though there was a cramp in it.

"All the way to hell."

"That's easy," said the Slogger. "Sure, I'd go."

"Is he as white as that?"

"Him?" said the Slogger. "White? They didn't know what white meant until he came along. They named white after him. There ain't no white man except him."

"I like you, kid," said O'Rourke. "You've gotta spend a couple of days with us, maybe. That's all. We'll treat you good. You know why I like you? It's because I like Dick Willett."

"Yeah, do you?" said the Slogger. "Yeah, ain't he great, though?"

"How did he come to slip you the grand?"

75

"He backed me when I quit to Marley. I heard he was in town. I went to see him, even if he knew I'd been a dog. My kid was flat. I had to do something. Willett was the biggest guy I ever seen. I just sneaked up to his room. He pretty near threw me out. When he seen my back, he wilted. He gave me the handout. He fixed me at the Garden. There was a gun in the bureau drawer along with the money. He said drop it in my pocket. That's all. . . . I'm glad you like him, chief. I'd eat hell like honey if he told me to."

AFTERWARDS, O'Rourke and Campbell faced each other across a desk with bitter hatred in their eyes.

"He had the only face for murder in the lot," said Campbell. That's why I knew. And he spoke out too quick about the lamp shade. Right then I began to deduce. A face fit for murder and talk about lamp shades. Pretty far fetch between. He shouldn't know a lamp shade from a shovel. But he does. I figure him quick. He knows. He knows too much. He'd have the brain to do anything . . . even the switching of the lamp shades, even throwing the wire in Telford's front yard and. . . ."

"All we know is that a bird named Willett was carrying Morrison's gun. That's all we know, and you've got him hanged already. You're a nut, Campbell. You ain't serving justice. You're serving a grudge. The thing we do is to call on Willett and have a little look-see about what he says."

13

❖

"Willett Talks"

W illett was breakfasting in his room in a dressing gown. It was an old khaki-colored bit of silk, rubbed thin by much use. It fell away from his neck and showed all the multiple fingers of strength that ran toward his throat. He was as far as fruit and offered the silver dish of it to the detectives. Campbell took nothing. O'Rourke began to crunch an apple. At every crunch, the eyes of Campbell were pulled suddenly toward him with poisonous annoyance. He wished that he had taken something for himself but now he could not change his mind, he felt.

"Ever take an interest in a pug named Slogger Haines?" asked Campbell.

Willett worked on an orange with a spoon.

"Yes, I know the Slogger," he said.

"You know what detectives have to do . . . always asking questions," said Campbell. "It's a mean life, Mr. Willett. You don't mind us going around and around the block?"

"Not a bit. Hope you find the right house," said Willett.

"What's the last time you saw the Slogger?" asked Campbell.

"Just the other day," he said.

"Ah, you seen him just the other day," said Campbell. "Kind of hard to hear what you say, Sergeant O'Rourke makes so much noise. Well, you mind telling us how you found the Slogger?"

"Down. The Slogger was very down."

"Did you do anything about it?"

"I gave him a handout."

"Twenty bucks or so?"

"No," said Willett. "Twenty dollars doesn't give a fellow like Slogger a new start. It only gives him a drunk."

"You wanted to give him a new start?" asked O'Rourke.

"Yes."

"Mind telling us why? Win a lot of money on him in the old days?" asked Campbell.

"No, I lost money when he quit to Benny Marley five years ago. But once I needed a left-hook and remembered the Slogger."

"You needed a sock and needed it bad, eh? said O'Rourke.

"It made a lot of difference to me . . . and the other fellow. The Slogger had a beautiful left-hook. It came out of nowhere and rang bells," explained Willett.

"So you fixed him up pretty well?"

"I gave him a thousand dollars."

"Hai!" said Campbell, and whistled. "That's making it pretty big!"

"Poker money, you know," said Willett.

"Gave him the money and that was all?"

"Yes."

"You're sure, eh?" asked Campbell.

"Yes."

Campbell stood up and pointed.

"What about the Kelmsford automatic out of your bureau drawer?" he shouted suddenly.

"That was a Kelmsford, was it?" said Willett.

"Sit down and stop yelling," said O'Rourke to Campbell. "You don't buy anything here with loud talk."

Campbell snorted.

"I'll talk to *you,* later," he said. "Now, Mr. Willett, I'd like to know where you bought that gun."

"I didn't buy it."

"Oh, you didn't buy it? Is that so?"

"Yes, that's so."

"You know that people have to have a license for carrying concealed weapons?"

"I didn't carry it. I put it in the bureau drawer."

"I mean . . . not beating about the bush . . . but I mean, where did you get that automatic?"

"I picked it up," said Willett.

"In the gutter?" asked Campbell.

Willett said nothing. He finished his orange.

"Where the hell do you think you are, anyway?" demanded O'Rourke. "What he means to say is, 'where did you pick it up, Mr. Willett?'"

"Off a davenport."

"Ah? A davenport, eh?" said Campbell, sneering. "In some lady's parlor, I guess?"

"In a man's living room."

"Where was the room?" asked Campbell.

"At David Barry's house."

"Ah? On the night of the twenty-second?"

"No, the morning of the twenty-third."

"When? When on that morning?"

"After we had been asked into the house, and after we came out from Barry's bedroom."

"You found it lying on the davenport?"

"Yes."

"In full view, eh?"

"Between two cushions."

"Why did you take it? Did it belong to you?"

"No."

"Then why did you take it?"

"Because I was watching Mr. Murderer Telford."

"Watching him?"

"I'd spoken about the red lamp in that room and wondered if Barry were color-blind. Afterwards, you two very cleverly discovered that Telford was color-blind—that business of the tie."

"That made you think that Telford had killed Barry?"

"If he changed those lamp shades, he had a reason for it. He was trying to cover up something. That was enough for me. I don't need many reasons to make me suspect him."

"No friend of yours?"

"I hate his heart."

"You thought he'd feel that you'd drawn suspicion toward him?"

"I did."

"Why did you make the remark about the lamp in the first place?"

"I wasn't thinking of Telford, then. I was simply thinking, out loud, that I'd never noticed any color-blindness in Barry when I first knew him. You fellows worked out the Telford angle for yourselves."

"You gave us a strong lead there, Mr. Willett."

"Did I? I'm glad of it."

"Why do you hate Telford so much?"

"He's an underground worker, a cheat, a rat. I've known him for years. When he loses his temper, he never shows it . . . and he never forgets. He's got the memory of an elephant and the technique of a panther. But some day he's going to lose control and run amok. I thought the other morning that he might be about to run amok. So I picked up the gun."

"Lucky you happened to see it just then, wasn't it?"

"I thought so."

"If Telford came at you, I'd say that you're big enough to take care of yourself."

"He wouldn't come at me with his hands."

"Would he use a gun?"

"He would."

"Does he go around armed?"

"Always."

O'Rourke broke into the train of the questioning to say, "That's worth a note."

He made an entry in a book.

Campbell snarled silently at his partner. He said, "You

thought that because you started the color-blind business and then Telford showed up color-blind . . . you thought that might be enough to send him at your throat?"

"Yes, I thought so. I still think so. I kept that automatic in my pocket, pointing straight at Telford all the time. If he made a move, I intended to rip him in two."

Campbell wiped his bald forehead and head. He said, "What's your theory of the way Telford committed the crime?"

"I think Telford came to see Barry. Perhaps he was pinched for money. Perhaps he wanted to hurry up his wedding with Jacqueline Barry. And, when he married her, have the cash in his hands at once. He's always had wide-spreading schemes. He's the sort of an hombre that always needs plenty of ready cash. So he made up his mind to rub Barry out of the way. It was easy. The old man lived alone. So he went to Barry's house, found him about to go to bed. Starting to unlace his shoes, perhaps. Barry was the sort of a man who wouldn't let the visit of a friend keep him up. Barry had the nature of a selfish swine, except where the newspapers might take notice of him. I think that he listened to Telford while he was working on his shoes, and that Telford wrapped the window cord around his neck at that moment—perhaps when the old man was leaning down toward the floor to get at the laces. I think that there was a struggle, and the bedside lamp was knocked over. When Barry was dead, Telford went through with the rest of his plan."

"What plan?" asked Campbell.

"He'd planned to make the thing look like suicide. He carried Barry up to the balcony in the living room and dropped him over so that it would look like suicide. He went back to look at the bedroom and see if there were any signs of the struggle left. Perhaps that was when he noticed that the lamp had fallen. I suppose that the shade was broken. He may have tried to fix it. It wouldn't fix. He decided that he wouldn't leave a thing like that to call attention to the bedroom. He simply went into the next room and got the shade from the lamp there. That's my theory, and I think it's a damned good one. Don't you?"

"*I* do," said O'Rourke.

"I don't," snapped Campbell. "At any rate, you stick to that story . . . that you found the automatic between the cushions on the davenport? You stick to that?"

Willett stared at him.

"Sorry, Mr. Willett," said O'Rourke. "Awfully sorry. Campbell is Scotch or something and he don't know how to talk to a gentleman."

"Ah, you damned . . . ," began Campbell. Then he added, "You still afraid that Telford might take a crack at you?"

"Unless he's jailed. I suppose you people are waiting for him to take alarm and run from the country? He'll never do that until he's married the heiress."

"What about you and Miss Barry?" demanded the Scotchman, suddenly.

"I'm afraid I've given you all the spare time I can afford," said Willett.

"Sorry, Mr. Willett," said O'Rourke. "But he don't know how to talk to a gentleman. He can't help it. He never learned!"

14

❖

"I'll Burn the Truth
Out of You!"

"If," said O'Rourke, "you don't want to arrest Telford . . . Mr. Murderer Telford, as Willett calls him . . . suppose we take a look into Morrison's gun?"

"Aye, and pull the trigger on yourself," said Campbell. "Do you think I forget how you talked to Willett about me?"

"It's a queer thing about me," answered O'Rourke, "I've got a pride in the force. I hate to see any member of it make a fool of himself and the whole rest of us."

"Rotten graft is more your line," declared Campbell. "Rotten picking of pockets on the side, taking the money out of greasy damned hands of politicians and what not."

O'Rourke laughed at him.

"You'll have a good time working up my case, one day," answered O'Rourke. "It's interesting. It's the way I've turned the corners so fast. You'll get dizzy tryin' to foller me around some of them. But lookin' at Morrison, what have we got?"

"His gun on the Barry davenport, if you believe your lying friend Willett."

"What makes you think he was lying?"

"He was too smooth. Naturally, he's rough. But he talked smooth. He didn't swear. You take a rough fellow and there's nothing that polishes him up so much as having to tell a lie. It kind of brings him together, like he was passing an examination. He talks book talk. Willett was pretty near doing that."

"Looking at Morrison," persisted O'Rourke, wearily, "we

83

see that his gun was at the Barry place. Do you admit that?"

"How do I know that Willett and Morrison aren't working in cahoots?"

"Maybe."

"Willett comes suddenly back East from the West. A couple of days later the man he used to work for, for five years, is dead. Funny, isn't it?"

"Yeah, it's a Scotch joke," said O'Rourke. "But just supposing, to please me, that the gun was found there . . . when did it get there? Did Morrison have it in his pocket that morning? Or, what about him being there the night before?"

"He alibis himself out of that. He was with Rose Taylor. She tells us that. It's got to be that way until we prove different."

O'Rourke nodded.

"He was out at the Barry house the night of the twenty-second," said O'Rourke "Suppose that he gets there, with a grudge against Barry. . . ."

"Why should he have a grudge?"

"Everybody hated Barry, and Morrison was his partner."

"Go on from there."

"It works out like this: Barry is in Morrison's way. Morrison goes out there to argue with him. He argues so hard that he pulls the Kelmsford automatic out of his pocket and waves it around . . . by the way, what's the report of the ballistic expert on the bullet that knocked over Pollok? Telephone and see, Angus."

Campbell pulled the telephone to him and made the call. The palm of his hand itched and he kept rubbing it on the edge of his desk. When his brain was fevered, he could not help that gesture.

"You got as far as Morrison waving the gun around. Then what?"

"Then he thinks of the noise the gun would make. He sees the scrawny throat of Barry and finishes the job the silent way."

"Hello . . . Dr. Callas?" said Campbell over the phone. "Got anything on the Pollok bullet? A which? All right. Thanks."

84

"Callas is up to date," said Campbell, turning from the telephone. He still rubbed his palm on the edge of the desk. "Pollok was knocked over by a bullet from a Kelmsford! Do we get Rose and Morrison and ask them a few questions?"

"Get the girl," said O'Rourke. "I'll collect Mr. Morrison . . . but, mind you, Angus, Telford was the man who murdered Barry."

CAMPBELL SAID, "You sit down here and make yourself comfortable, Miss Taylor."

She was wearing a white linen dress with a broad collar and a blue necktie. She had on very sensible, broad-toed shoes, made for walking distances. They made her feet remarkably small, but Campbell did not notice that. He never liked backgrounds. Clothes were background, so far as Angus Campbell was concerned.

"We want to find out about the night of the twenty-second," said Campbell.

Rose bowed her head a little and blushed.

"You remember the twenty-second, all right?" said Campbell. "That was the evening that Morrison came up to your place with the lobster and the champagne?"

"Yes," she said.

"If he hadn't been there, where would you have been?" asked Campbell.

Her smile was very faint and wondering, her eyes very wide.

"Listen, sister," said Campbell. "I'm not an O'Rourke. The baby eyes and all of that don't buy a thing with me. We know the truth, but we want to get the straight of it from you. I'm giving you a chance to help yourself. Now, tell me true, was Morrison with you the night of the twenty-second?"

"Oh, yes," said Rose.

"You lie," said Campbell.

She closed her eyes. She waited. As he stared at her, he could not detect the slightest bit of alteration in her expression.

"Ah!" said Campbell.

85

He looked around the room. It was small. There was this chair in which Rose sat, and one opposite which he occupied. Besides, there were half a dozen chairs lined up against the back wall. He got up, went to the window, and pulled the shade half down. He swung out from a corner a sort of traveling crane which supported what looked like a large camera. This he focused on the girl.

He said, "I'm gonna give you some light to see your own mind by." And he pulled a switch. A glare as of twenty search-lights beat into the face of the girl. She dropped her head forward.

"Do I have to tie you into that chair and rope your head in place, or will you face that light?"

She faced it.

"I can't keep my eyes open," she said.

"Sure you can't. You'll see the light right through the lids, just the same. Now, will you talk?"

"I *have* talked," she said.

"You still say that Morrison was with you?"

Her eyelids were beginning to redden; a tangle of small veins stood out on them. She trembled. She took a firm hold on the arms of the chair.

"Yes, Mr. Morrison was with me."

"It's a lie! You poor little fool," said Campbell, "the big fat stiff has come clean already. That night we know where he was!"

"He was with me," said Rose.

"You want me to tell you where he was? He was at the house of David Barry!"

The heat of the light was reddening her entire face. She did not start or gasp. She simply said, "He was with me till about ten."

"You're hard, ain't you?" demanded Campbell. "You think you're hard. But I'm going to keep you under the light, here, till it burns your brains dry and makes you tell the truth. Why do you want to lie? Morrison's turned you down. You're nothing to him. He told us so. He told us he was at Barry's house. Why do you want to lie like this? I'll keep you here on the spot for ten hours if I have to."

She sighed and was silent. Her eyes closed and her lips trembled.

He watched the small beads of sweat collecting on her forehead, and on the backs of her hands. Her lips were turning gray and dry.

Sometimes the biggest of men and the most resolute cracked after ten seconds of the brain-searing light. Closed eyelids merely reddened a little that terrible brightness that searched the soul. But the girl sat impassive. He had not had to touch her. He could swear, afterwards, that he had not touched her. If she chose to face the light merely because he told her to, that was her lookout. Her head lifted a little to one side. But still she faced the light.

"Will you talk?" said Campbell.

She said nothing. Her lips were parted. Thin lines of trouble, like pencilings of shadow, appeared between her eyes. He watched the quickened lifting of her linen dress across the breast. It flamed like a brilliant white fire. He could see the delicate shadow which the material cast, and some of the flesh on which the shadow fell—a shadow within a flame.

Perhaps she was about to faint?

"Ten hours, if I have to," said Campbell, "will you talk?"

She said nothing.

The door opened. The voice of O'Rourke said, "This is pretty. This is pretty Scotch!"

He came over and turned off the light. Darkness in a wave washed across the room; then the softer daylight resumed by degrees.

O'Rourke said through his teeth, "Why . . . damn you!"

Campbell did not answer. Somehow he felt that he might have done wrong, though of course a detective honestly bent on serving the cause of truth hardly can do wrong.

O'Rourke squatted on his heels. He took out a clean handkerchief and with it wiped the sweating face of the girl. He took her hands one by one and wiped them, also. She kept her eyes closed.

"How are you, Rose?" asked O'Rourke.

"I'm all right, Sergeant O'Rourke," she said.

"If you want to turn in a complaint about this sort of treatment that you've had, I'll take you to the chief," said O'Rourke.

"I don't want to complain," she said.

"Did you hear that?" he demanded.

"Yeah, I heard it," said Campbell. "She wouldn't talk. I would have burned the truth out of her, if you hadn't stepped in. She's all right. She's not touched."

"Stand up," said O'Rourke. "Can you stand up?"

She stood.

"Now, try opening your eyes."

She opened them and smiled upwards at O'Rourke.

"Thank you," she said.

15

❖

"Another Suspect Talks"

Morrison said, "What are you going to do? None of the hard-boiled stuff with me, boys, or I'll break the lot of you. I know where to put in a word that will sink the toughest of you!"

O'Rourke looked down at the flat of his hand. Then he struck Morrison as hard as he could across the face with the palm. Morrison staggered. His knees hit the edge of the chair and he sat down with a thud.

"Tie him into the chair," said O'Rourke.

Campbell put a noose of rope around Morrison.

"Go on!" gasped Morrison. "Go on! My God, you'll spend twenty years in the pen. You'll go up the river for this. And you'll never come down again. I know how to keep a lad in the cool as long as I please. I'm going to break you both and. . . ."

O'Rourke lifted his hand and looked at it again. Morrison stopped talking.

"I ain't had any exercise for a long time, Angus," said O'Rourke. "I'm gonna make up by beating hell out of this big stiff . . . or do you feel like talking? Where were you the night of the twenty-second?"

"I've told you already. I was with Rose Taylor."

"You lie," said O'Rourke. "I'm gonna sock you right in your dirty mouth for telling that lie and, if you start spitting blood and teeth on the floor, I'm gonna sock you again. . . . When I beat your teeth loose, you swaller them, you understand?"

He poised himself, rising a little on his toes.

Morrison ducked back his head.

"Wait a minute!" he said.

"He's yellow, all right," observed Campbell.

"I don't care whether he's yellow or not," said O'Rourke, "I'm gonna beat hell out of him, unless he tells the whole story."

"What story do you want?" asked Morrison. The hands of O'Rourke fascinated him. He could not help staring at them. And he kept pursing and parting his lips and there was a whistle in his breathing.

"Look at that mug," said O'Rourke. "What a sandbag that would be to sock! I want the story of what you did the night of the twenty-second. Start about you and the Kelmsford automatic."

Morrison's head dropped. His bulk shuddered like jelly.

At last he said, "I give it up. It's no use. . . . And she told you that I wasn't with her?"

"She did," said Campbell.

"Don't lie," broke in O'Rourke. "She didn't say a word. She stuck by the guns through hell. And hell was what she got. She didn't blat a word. Everything you say, you're saying by yourself." He added, "Take the rope off him, Angus. I only hope he makes a move so I can slam him. Now, talk, you fat rat. You and the Kelmsford, what did you do, the night of the twenty-second?"

Campbell said, "Wait a minute. We might take a look through his office." He winked at O'Rourke. Then he added, "Let's have your office keys."

"Have you got a search warrant?" asked Morrison, sadly.

"You want us to get one?" demanded Campbell.

Morrison pulled a bunch of keys out of his pocket.

"Here you are," he said.

"Tell us what they are?"

"Locker at the club. House key. Kennel key. Boathouse key. Country club locker," said Morrison. "Here's the office key. Safe in the office. Key to. . . ."

90

"That's enough," said Campbell, and seized on the bunch of keys and left the room.

O'Rourke settled down. He lighted one of the cigars. His eyes kept traveling all over the face and body of Morrison. The big man was sick in heart and mind. He could not meet the inquiry of that eye.

"Go on," said O'Rourke. "Start early in the evening."

"Barry was a hard man," said Morrison. "He always was hard. He put on a good front for the newspapers, but he was hard. After he started into the partnership with me, either he was always asking questions, or he was sending his lawyer to ask questions."

"Who was his lawyer?" demanded O'Rourke.

"John Telford."

"That's right. Go on. Keep right on the track all the way through."

"I'm glad to," said Morrison. "It gets something off my chest. You'd had to know, sooner or later. Well, that evening I drove out to Barry's house while it was still light."

"While it was still what?"

"It was still light. I went in to see Barry and have it out with him. He'd started talking like a fool. He'd started talking about an investigation."

"Investigation of what?"

"You know, in doing business in a big way, you don't count every penny. You don't catch your pennies and tag them before they fly away in the autumn and see how many come back the next spring. If you're gonna do big things, you do 'em in a big way. Got another cigar?"

"Sure," said O'Rourke. "I been mean enough with you, big boy. Here you are. How do you like it?"

"It's good," said Morrison. He puffed at the cigar. "A man of your age and experience understands the way things go, O'Rourke. You can't have the world with a fence around it. Sometimes you pull down the fence and let people move in on your land, a ways. It pays in the long run."

"I know," said O'Rourke. "Otherwise you get the grease put under you."

"Yeah, and don't you? Take a man of the world like you, you can understand. Take a pinch-faced rat like Barry; what could he understand? Nothing! He got to talking and threatening. Finally I said to myself that I'd talk to him. If I couldn't talk to him, I'd bluff him. Well, I went out there and tried to talk like a human being, and it didn't do any good. I had to swallow insults. A man like me couldn't swallow insults. I tried the bluff. I pulled out the gun. He sat back with a thin kind of a sneer. He looked dirty. I put the gun down and tried to change his mind. I couldn't change his mind. He didn't have a mind to change. He only had a cash register. Well, I never did like a cash register. I had a brain that worked and it made money, and that was that."

"Go on," said O'Rourke. "I like the way you tell it. How'd you ever happen to be a partner of Barry's?"

"Telford's a good fellow," said Morrison. "When he got to handling Barry's business he said to me, once, that Barry and me ought to get together. He had the money and I had the ways of investing it at something better than five percent."

"I can understand that," said O'Rourke. "Go ahead."

16

❖

"Trail of Fear"

After a while the telephone rang and O'Rourke picked it up. Campbell was saying, "I've looked things over. There's nothing even in the safe except junk, and a ledger. But the ledger may say what we want to know. It's the accounts of the Barry–Morrison partnership business. And the figures are big."

"We'd better have that," said O'Rourke.

"You think I could sneak it and put an accountant at work on it? You think I could take it out of the office and have one of the lads work it over?"

"Have it done there," said O'Rourke.

"You mean, call an accountant in here to work the thing over?"

"Yes. I mean that."

"Will you take care of Morrison for a couple of hours?"

"Yes, or more."

"Going far into things?"

"Pretty far. So long," said O'Rourke.

He turned back to his questioning.

"So you just drove back home after that?"

"Yes. I drove back into town."

"Feeling sort of seedy, about that time? Stop for a drink?"

"I went over to the apartment of Rose. You know about that, so why shouldn't I talk? I went there but she wasn't in."

"Oh, she wasn't in, eh?"

"No, she wasn't in. You can't keep a girl like that locked up, and I wouldn't be a fool to try."

"She's straight enough, anyway," answered O'Rourke.

"Yeah, and you're right, she is. She knows which side her bread is buttered on, and she knows what butter is, too. Rose is all right."

"Sure she is. She's a sweet kid," said O'Rourke. "She wouldn't run around with more than one at once."

"She wouldn't be such a fool," said Morrison. "She knows what I am in this town. Nobody knows better than Rose does."

"Kind-hearted kid, ain't she?" asked O'Rourke. "Kind to a fellow by name of Pollok, that was killed the other day?"

"Pollok? She introduced me to him. Poor boy that's always been sick and sort of set back in his work. I did a couple of things for him. Set him on his feet, you know. Yes, Rose was that sort of girl. I'll tell you . . . she was the sort of girl that never forgot a friend. I've seen tears in her eyes . . . when she went by some poor stiff, I've seen tears in her eyes! That's the kind of a girl that she is."

O'Rourke started out of his chair and thundered suddenly, "Then why did you go and shoot him through the head with a Kelmsford automatic?"

"Me?" gasped Morrison. "Hey, what do you mean?"

"You bought two of those guns. And a Kelmsford was used on Pollok. Where's your second gun, Morrison?"

"Mine? I lost it the other . . . oh, my God!" groaned Morrison. "What are you talking about?"

"You lost it, eh? Where did you lose it? Answer out!"

"I didn't . . . I mean it was in my office and it disappeared. I don't know how it could have. . . . O'Rourke, what are you trying to do to me?"

O'Rourke suddenly began to laugh.

"Take it easy," he said. "You know how it is with us. We got to throw a bluff into the boys, now and then."

"Pollok!" said Morrison. "Shoot Pollok? My God, why would I shoot Pollok?"

"That's what I want to know. Why would you? Sure you wouldn't?" said O'Rourke.

The door opened on Detective Sergeant Campbell. He said: "I want to see you, O'Rourke."

"Morrison didn't have anything to do with Pollok," said O'Rourke.

"I want to see you," said Campbell.

"Wait a minute, Mr. Morrison, and I'll be right back here with you," said O'Rourke.

He went out into the next little room with Campbell.

"I took Flynn up there with me," said Campbell. "When I finished talking with you over the phone, Flynn had heard me and he said that *he* had been trained as a public accountant, but the work was too cramping for him."

"He wanted the big, open spaces so he got into the force, eh?" O'Rourke grinned.

"I told Flynn to hop to it. I settled into a ledger that we found in the safe. In five minutes he whistled. In ten minutes he was standing up pointing something out to me. There was a mistake in a mighty small thing. Mistake in addition. You know what the mistake was?"

"How would I know? I never added straight in my life."

"Just the mistake of including the cents with the dollars. It turned a hundred and seventy-five into seventeen thousand five hundred."

"Ai, ai, ai!" murmured O'Rourke. "And I've always thought that a fellow like Morrison would have brains, even if he was a yellow skunk."

"Sure you would," said Campbell. "You got no more sense. Every crook looks like a wise man till he gets behind the bars. We'll go in and have a talk with Morrison about bookkeeping."

They went back into the next room. There was not a soul in the place. The door was ajar. The corridor beyond was empty. Morrison was gone.

O'Rourke shouted, "Why, the damn fool . . . why, is he trying to make a sucker out of me? Is he trying to run out on me?"

He jumped for the telephone.

"What's the matter?" asked Campbell.

"What's the matter? Why, I'm going to turn in an alarm on him. He can't get away with this. I'm going to. . . ."

"Look fine for the inspector to know we can't keep our hands on the birds we catch, won't it?" asked Campbell.

"Aye . . . damn it . . . he's ridden me for that before!" said O'Rourke.

"Wait a minute," said Campbell. "I'll fix that."

He took the telephone and lighted a cigarette as he said: "Give me the radio . . . Sergeant Campbell speaking . . . tell the nearest radio car in the East Fifties to go to this address. . . . Wait a minute, here it is." He spelled out the address.

"Tell them to go up to the apartment on the third floor and arrest the man they'll find there. There'll be a girl, too, but let the girl go. We only want the man. Tell the car to report to me by wire." He hung up and then sat down in a chair.

"It looks bad, Pat," he admitted. "Telford, Willett, Jacqueline Barry, and now Morrison. Four we got, and the four make nothing at all!"

"Four? What have you got on Willett?"

"We'll have plenty before long. I'm working on his trail all by myself, Pat. Leave Willett to me. Hai, but there's a fog we're walking through now, Pat. Do you see your hand before your face in this case?"

"Damned if I do," agreed O'Rourke.

And then, minutes later, he was muttering, "Would Morrison go straight out to Rose's place?"

"I think he would. When the big ones are soft, they always go to a woman in a pinch," answered Campbell.

The telephone rang hard on the heels of the last word. A big, booming voice came over the wire to Campbell, "We've got a man here who says he's Jay Wainwright, but the cards on him say that he's Jeffrey Morrison."

"Bring him in," said Campbell.

He turned to O'Rourke.

"Knowing about women, that's what makes it easy for me to turn tricks in this business. You'd be a fine detective, O'Rourke . . . you'd be a great detective, except that the women turn you into a soggy bum."

17

❖

"Rose Makes an Offer"

When Rose Taylor got to Willett's hotel, she found that he was gone and left a forwarding address for mail only and not for inquiry.

"Oh, but then I have to go home without seeing him?" said Rose.

Whenever she looked up without smiling, it was for a definite reason. Now it was plain that a friendless world confronted her. The clerk was even more human than most. He scribbled a few words on a piece of paper.

"Of course Mr. Willett wanted to make exceptions," said he.

That was how Rose found herself, half an hour later, at the door of an old brownstone front. Before she pressed the bell she listened, because Rose was a girl who did things according to systems, and one of her systems was first to listen even if she could not look. Inside the house she heard, or rather felt, a regular, heavy pulsation, as though a badly oiled or very ponderous machine were turning.

After she had pressed the bell, the door was partly opened by a low-built, wide man in a sweater. He had only three wrinkles of flesh between his eyebrows and his hair, which was a downpouring shag of darkness.

"Yeah?" he said.

"Mr. Willett?" she asked, with her upward smile.

"Huh!" said he. "He ain't here."

"May I wait for him?" she asked.

"No," said the man.

Her eyes touched on the back of one of his huge, dangling hands.

"But haven't I seen you somewhere in the ring?" she asked.

"Yeah?" said he. "Where?"

"I don't know. In some crowded place, knocking someone out. In the Garden, was it?"

"No, it wasn't in the Garden," he said. "Who are you?"

"Rose Taylor."

"How long ago you see it?"

"Oh, quite a long time."

"Maybe it was Gypsy Morgan," said he.

"Maybe that was the name. A great big man."

"He looked bigger than he was. He couldn't take it. Whatcha want with the governor?"

"He asked me if I could possibly come to see him today. I thought he said to come at this time, too."

"Yeah, he's late," said the Slogger. "But nobody's to come in. What looking sort of a guy was the one you seen me K.O.?"

"Huge, and . . . rather horrible looking."

"He wasn't as horrible as he looked. That long jaw was made to order, what I mean. . . . Nobody's to come in. Sorry. I ain't to let anybody in."

At this, she laughed.

"Of course not," she said, "except me."

"Except what?" asked the Slogger.

He raised his eyebrows. His forehead disappeared.

"Well . . . I think he'll expect me to be here," she said, and she blushed.

"You think he'll . . . oh!" said the Slogger.

He looked over his shoulder. No advice came from the rear.

"Well," said the Slogger, "I wouldn't know. . . ."

"I don't like to wait on the street," she said. "That might make Dick angry. And you know when he loses his temper."

"Yeah, and don't I know," said the Slogger, looking upward. "Wait a minute . . . well, come on in. What harm could it do, anyway?"

"I don't know," said Rose.

He stepped back. She saw that he had in his other hand a skipping rope. He closed the door behind her. The hallway was dim. He opened another door. The Victorian darkness of the place was only a mask. All the rear end of the first floor was a great, high room paneled in pine, with a soft, pale rug on the floor, and bound books for color along the walls. The windows were curtained in printed linen, and the same sort of linen covered the davenport and some of the deep chairs. The taint of pipe smoke kept in the air. It seemed to Rose a pleasant smell. On the table beside the largest chair there was a rack of pipes.

"What a nice room," said Rose.

"Friend of the governor owns it," said the Slogger.

"It's just the sort of a room to fit Dick," said the girl.

"Yeah, and ain't it?" said the Slogger. He extended a great hand in an explanatory gesture. "It's got a kind of a who's-it, ain't it?"

"It's big," said Rose.

"You couldn't house that guy in a coop, could you?" asked the Slogger.

"He's the biggest man I know," said Rose.

"You and me," said the Slogger. He sat down on the edge of a wooden chair. "You and him old friends?" he asked.

"You don't have to be old to be friends with Dick," said she.

There was the sound of a door opening, slamming. A draught sucked over the threshold of the library.

"That's he!" cried Rose. "Shall I run and surprise him?"

"Wait a minute . . . wait a minute," said the Slogger. "How would I know that he wants to be surprised? He ain't a guy to be surprised."

He opened the door.

"Hello, chief," he said. "She's here!"

Willett came suddenly, rapidly, through the door, brushing past the Slogger. He looked at Rose before he had taken off his hat.

"Ah, ha!" he said, and took the hat off.

"This was the time you said to come, wasn't it?" asked Rose.

"Did I?" asked Willett. He gave his hat to the Slogger. "Put this away and bring me something to drink, will you, Slogger?" he asked.

"I was all right letting her in?" asked the Slogger.

"Get me something to drink," repeated Willett.

He went over to the girl. She started to stretch out her hand. He offered her a cigarette case.

"No, thank you," she said.

He took one and lighted it. Then he went over to one of the big windows and stared out of it.

"Are you angry, Mr. Willett?" she asked.

He kept on smoking, silently.

The Slogger came in with a tray. He put it down, and stared with wonder at the silent back of Willett. Then he scowled a bitter question at the girl. She laid a finger on her lips and shook her head at the Slogger, laughing. But he went out of the room, dubiously, glowering at her again as he closed the door.

She poured a stiff Scotch into one of the tall glasses and went over to Willett. She stood just beside and behind him.

"Well, if you think you've got something, what is it?" he asked.

"Whiskey," she said.

He turned around and took the glass.

"Ah?" said Willett. He took a good swallow without blinking.

"Do you drink a lot, Dick?" she asked.

At this, he lifted his head a little. In repose his face was always stern. It was a little more stern than usual, just now.

"I drink a little to make the smoke taste better," he said. He took another swallow. "What's it about?"

"It's terrible to be alone in New York, don't you think?" she asked.

"Are you alone?" said Willett.

101

"I am; and terribly lonely. I always have been."

"Sit down, Rose. I see it's going to be a long talk."

She went to a chair but merely stood beside it, waiting.

"Stop looking that way," he said. "Whatever you are, you're not afraid."

"I'd learn to look new ways," said Rose. She put a hand up to her hair. The loose of the sleeve fell back from her arm. She was wearing blue silk that flowed into watery lights. "That's the point, Dick . . . I could learn. I'm not stupid. I've simply been with stupid men."

"Will you have a drink?" he asked.

She poured a taste into a glass and squirted a foam of siphon into it.

"To you . . . Dick," she said.

He said nothing. Then he went to a chair and sat down. She slipped down onto the arm of hers and sat there poised, watching him. The sun, slanting through the high windows, burned on the glass she held, and on her hair.

"Well, go on," said Willett.

"I thought that it might do," she said, "because you like me a little, don't you?"

"And you've made up your mind?" he said.

She looked up with her smile.

"Don't do that, damn it," said Willett.

She rubbed the tips of her fingers over her eyes, over her smile.

"There . . . it's gone," she said. "I'd learn quickly, too," she added. "If you could have a little patience."

"Go on talking," said Willett.

"About us?"

"I suppose so."

"Well, you like me already. You've no idea how much more you'd like me in time. I could be a decoration, couldn't I? I could be a help, too." She was using her eyes again.

"You think you're serious?"

"I think so."

"It's a new world and all that, eh?"

"Yes . . . I mean, I feel a bit misty and I hate everything in my apartment. I never met. . . ." Here she paused. "You see how quickly I can learn?" she asked, smiling.

"You're a clever little devil," said Willett. "But why all this?"

"I don't know. I never thought that I was really ambitious, till I met you."

"You think it would be a pretty high flight?"

"I know it would."

"If there were a crash, you'd need a parachute."

She merely smiled. "That's all right," she said.

"Sorry," said Willett, "but it's no go."

"No?"

"Sorry," he said.

"Because I've been around a good deal; does that disgust you? I haven't been around such a great lot, though. But does it disgust you?"

"Not very much. Are you saying good-bye?"

She sipped her drink. Willett said, "I thought so. There's some other way of taking hold of the problem. Let's hear what you have to say."

"I don't want to talk about it," she said.

"You will, though," said he.

"Do you have to be so hard all the time?" she asked.

"Carry on, Rose," he told her.

"It's because I think that afterwards you'd come to like me. You know, Dick, you think of me being a silky little cat. I'm not so little, either. I'm five-feet-five. I'm not one of those huge girls, but I'm strong. You think about battering around the world on horses, or mules, or tramp freighters, and how soon I would rub out or wash away?

"Well, I've worn overalls, and I could do it again. I've cooked at a campfire, and I could do it again. I've shot venison and I could shoot again. You'd get so used to me that you wouldn't know what to do if you misplaced me. I'm that sort of a girl, at heart. I'm not just a damned little fool. How does all that check with you?"

"All right," said Willett. "Let's get down to bedrock, though."

"This is where I make or break, isn't it?" she said, looking up at the ceiling. "I hope I don't break! Well, it's about that night at the Barry house . . . the night of the twenty-second. I mean, about you being there. . . . Does that make you angry?"

"Every good cat is a hunter," said Willett. "No, it doesn't make me angry. Who was with you?"

"Sid Pollok."

"Who else was seen entering the house?"

"Morrison and Jacqueline Barry."

"Sit down and be comfortable," said Willett. "I knew we had to have quite a talk."

18

❖

"A Damp Coat—and
a Girl"

The voice over the telephone said: "Willett has gone to his apartment. He's just gone there."

"Stick and watch," said Campbell, and hung up.

He turned about in the swivel chair.

"Your story is that you didn't leave your house that night at all, Mr. Telford?" he said.

"I've told you that before."

O'Rourke said, "It's not the truth, though. Sorry, Mr. Telford. There's a coat hanging in your hall closet, a heavy tweed. It was still damp, yesterday. And the only rain for a long time was the night of the twenty-second, after dark."

"Ah, you found the coat, did you?" said Telford. He lifted his fine head and smiled straight at O'Rourke. "Naturally I wouldn't admit that I'd been outside, that night."

"Why would you admit it?" asked O'Rourke.

"The whole world knows that I'm to marry Jacqueline Barry and that she is practically the sole heiress of the Barry millions. Besides, I live close to the Barry house."

"How did you get out in the rain?" asked Campbell. "Wait a minute," he added, as the telephone rang again.

Over the wire there was a voice saying, "Sergeant O'Rourke? Sergeant O'Rourke?"

"No, Campbell."

"This is Bennett. Get this quick. Jacqueline Barry is in town, touring around. She's in a shop just now, and I get this chance to report. Riding this morning. Spot of tennis after lunch. Then she came for town in her car like a bat out of hell. The cops know her and wave her along, but I nearly killed myself keeping her in sight. Her hand is faster than my eye. I may lose her in this town traffic. That's all. So long."

Campbell turned back.

"The question was, how did you happen to get out in the rain that night?"

"That's easy. I sat up late in my study, working. I was about to go to bed when I had an idea that I'd left my old briefcase in the garage. There wasn't anything very important in it, but I went out."

"Was it there?"

"Yes. In the backseat of the car. I came back inside."

"Right into the house?"

"No, I was tired from working so long. Wrinkles in the brain, you know. I faced the rain and let it blow into my face for a while. It felt good. It reminded me of being a youngster and out in the rain with a scolding waiting at home. You know, the way a youngster feels, sometimes."

"Then you went inside?"

"Yes."

"That business about the changed lamp shade and you being color-blind," said Campbell, with an air of great frankness, "is a bit against you, Mr. Telford."

"I know it is."

"What do you think . . . now that we're being frank, all of us . . . about the lamp shade business?"

"I think a great deal about it. Do you remember the first voice that mentioned the lamp shade and color-blindness?"

"No," said O'Rourke. "Who was it?"

"A man who isn't an interior decorator, by any means. Willett!" He clicked his teeth on the name.

"What do you make out of Willett's mentioning it?"

"I don't know. But it struck me hard that he wasn't the sort of man to talk about the color of furniture."

"I thought so, too," said Campbell, sympathetically. "Did you notice it right away and feel a bit hard about Willett?"

"I did."

"Damned hard?" asked O'Rourke.

"I couldn't keep my eyes off him." said Telford.

"When there was that business about the neckties, did you notice Willett?" asked Campbell.

"I always notice him."

"He was standing by the davenport, wasn't he?" asked O'Rourke.

Campbell glanced at the other detective.

"No," said Telford. "He never was near the davenport."

Campbell said, quickly, "Are you sure of that?"

"Absolutely certain."

"Never near the davenport at all?"

"I'll take an oath about that," said Telford.

"Never mind the oath," said O'Rourke. "You don't like Willett, eh?"

"When you were a youngster," said Telford, "did you ever read books about the prairie Indians?"

"Yes."

"They were made out to be a wonderful lot. They could read a trail like the print in a book, eh?"

"That's right," nodded Campbell.

"Cruel devils," went on Telford. "If they caught you, the killing was slow and they enjoyed the taste of every moment of it. They could shoot an antelope at six hundred yards. They could tell the weather by the wind. They were stronger than most people. They could stalk a wild cat and catch it asleep."

"I remember all that stuff," said O'Rourke. "They were like some of these book detectives that Campbell admires so damn much. They were always deducin', too."

"Well," said Telford, "Willett is one of those prairie Indians in a white skin. I've known him since he was a boy."

"Have you?" said O'Rourke. "Mean guy, was he?"

Telford became thoughtful. He leaned forward, hands on his knees.

"It's like this," he said. "Willett *is* a red Indian. And the Indians had friends, you know. Inside the tribe there never were any murders. They'd die for one another. Only the enemies were to be killed from ambuscade, or knifed in the back, and the women and children slaughtered along with the men. One scalp was as good as another."

"And Willett's that way?" asked Campbell, full of interest.

"I'm saying, a great deal," said Telford. "Frankly . . . I hate the man. But I'm trying to give you a true picture. There's nothing nobler than a man who will die for a friend. Well, the truth is that I feel Willett would die for a friend . . . in a minute. Go through hell for a friend. Like the red Indian of the old books. But an enemy . . . that's exactly the opposite. Against an enemy, he'd scheme and plot for ten years for the sake of doing him in. He has the craft of . . . well, the craft of a woman, when he's out to make trouble. The patience of a hunting cat. The venom of a snake. The cleverness of the devil himself! That sounds a lot, but I won't take back a word. . . . I remember him when he was a sophomore in a football game and the tackle opposite him roughed him up a lot. Two years later he went West and played that same team on their own grounds. The same tackle in there against Willett. . . ."

"You mean that Willett knocked him out?" asked Campbell.

Telford shook his head. "I'll tell you what happened," he explained. "Willett spent the whole first quarter working on the other fellow. In the second quarter he told the quarterback to drive through right tackle every time he needed yards. And every time, the yards were made. After half-time it was the same thing. Willett was torturing that other tackle, making a fool of him, turning him yellow, robbing him of the hard work of four seasons. In the third period, the other coach saw that nothing would do and started warming up a substitute tackle. And that was when the crash came. Willett couldn't play with his mouse any more . . . his two–hundred–and–twenty–pound mouse . . . so he smashed him flat. Ribs. Three ribs. But it was more than broken bones. I never saw that tackle but I know what he is today. He asks your pardon before he even starts to say that he thinks the weather is good. I wonder if you begin to get my picture of Willett?"

"I get it," snapped Campbell.

"Then I'll say one thing more. Willett hates me more than he ever hated any other man."

O'Rourke was lighting a cigar, turning it carefully in the flame.

Campbell said, "You think that Willett is trying to frame you in some way?"

Telford thought again. He answered, "He'd spend five years of life to give me five days of trouble."

"Being a red Indian, he wouldn't care whether he got any other profit out of you?" asked O'Rourke.

"Being a white-skinned man," said Telford, "he'd think of profit, too."

"What extra profit would he get out of smashing you?" asked O'Rourke.

"Anything that's nearest my heart and pocketbook," said Telford

"What's nearest your heart and pocketbook?" asked Campbell. He looked at the smoke that Telford was blowing, fascinated by his inward thought. Then he insisted, "What's he doing while you're talking to the police about a wet overcoat?"

"I know!" Telford exclaimed. "He's with Jacqueline Barry this moment!"

"The hell he is!" said O'Rourke.

Telford made a gesture with both hands. He added, "I don't mean exactly that. Of course I don't mean exactly at this instant. But how could he hurt me more? Where's the vulnerable point at this moment? It's the girl I'm engaged to, and I'll swear . . . why didn't I think of it before? . . . that he's working some damned device in his red Indian brain!"

"You think he's lost his heart to Miss Barry?" asked Campbell.

"His heart?" Telford laughed. "My God, Campbell, the

man *hasn't* any heart! How could he lose it?"

The telephone rang again. Campbell answered it.

"Hello! Hello!" said a booming voice over the wire. "O'Rourke?"

"No, Campbell."

"This is hot," said the voice. "I'm Bennett. I got on her trail again, all right. A hard dodge of it, but I followed her on to her destination. Where do you think? The apartment that Willett took. The new one. You told me about it. She's just gone into the old house! What shall I do now?"

"Stick around there and use your eyes and ears," said Campbell. "Maybe you'll get some help before long."

He put up the telephone and turned, looking for a long moment at O'Rourke. He smiled as he looked. Campbell said, "Mr. Telford, suppose that you were right and that your friend Willett and Miss Barry were together just now . . . what would you think about it?"

"I wouldn't have to think!" said Telford through his teeth.

O'Rourke growled, "Hold on, Angus!"

"Why should I hold on?" demanded Campbell. "The natural way is mostly the best way. Show the set-up and then let nature take its course, I'd say. Suppose we want to have Telford talk to Willett face to face, just now. You and me along to keep off the violence? Well, come along, the two of you. There'll be a chance to do some seeing *and* some talking."

He began to laugh softly.

19

❖

"A Spot of Green Paint"

Finally Willett said, "Well, what does it all add up to?"
Rose said, "It adds up to this; you should take another drink."

"That's the sum, is it?" Willett smiled, and he filled his glass.

"You shouldn't drink that," said the girl, "unless you're going to have a long sleep afterward."

"I won't have a long sleep," answered Willett. "I never have a long sleep. Why do you think I shouldn't drink this?"

"Because I'm never afraid of men, but I'm afraid of you, now," she told him.

"We were talking about something else," said Willett.

"Yes," she said.

"You tell me what it was. Tell me in words of one syllable."

"We were wondering if I could make you happy," she said.

"Hell, no! We weren't wondering at all. I know you could," said Willett.

"Then, we don't have to talk any more. It's ended," she said.

"The fact is, Rose," said Willett, "that the whole thing is a bust."

"You don't have to say anything," she told him. "I'll go. I'll go now, Dick."

"Why do you look at me as though I were going to murder you?" asked Willett.

"I'm not looking at you in any way. Good-bye, Dick," she said.

"Don't be a fool," said Willett.

111

"No. I won't be," said Rose.

"You wanted a reason. I'm going to give you one."

"Yes, Dick," she said.

"If you hadn't been out there watching the Barry house, the sky would have been the limit. But I hate guns, and you've got a gun at my head. Go ahead and pull the trigger."

"I won't do anything," she said. "I won't tell anybody. . . . I won't."

"Why are you cringing like that?" he asked. He walked up to her. "Do you think you're in danger . . . here . . . with me?"

"No!" gasped Rose.

"Open your eyes and look at me," said Willett.

"Yes," said the girl.

"Am I such a devil as all that?"

"No, Dick," she said.

"Then why do you look so sick?"

"I'm not sick. I won't look any way at all."

"Do you think I'm drunk?"

"No, Dick. I don't think so."

"I am, though," said Willett. "So it's time for you to go home."

He went out into the hall with her.

"Listen," said Willett. "Any other time I would have sky-rocketed. Understand? Skyrocketed! But just now you're only another girl. If you can gain anything through the stuff you've got on me, go ahead and use it. It's all you'll ever get out of me. I carry the white flower of the molly. I'm immune. D'you know what I mean?"

"Yes, I know," she said.

"I don't think you do," said he. "You know about Odysseus?"

"No," she said.

"It doesn't make any difference," said Willett. He opened the front door. "Good-bye, Rose."

"Good-bye," she said, and slipped out.

He was closing the door when he saw that Jacqueline Barry was there on the front steps. She was hesitating, as though about to turn back. Rose Taylor spoke to her and hurried on. Jacqueline merely nodded. Then she made up her mind and came on toward the door.

Her green eyes were hard and clear.

"This isn't on the books," she said. "But is it all right for me to see you?"

He looked up the street toward Rose Taylor. She was walking quickly, hurrying as though she were late for an appointment, but he knew that she was only in haste to get far away from him. He smiled. Then he saw his smile taking effect on Jacqueline Barry.

"Are you coming in?" he asked, opening the door.

She stood there, eyeing him.

"I'm drunk, but not very," he stated. "Are you coming in, or not?"

She came in. He closed the door behind her.

"If I keep my breath away from you, you won't be conscious of the way I am," said Willett, "because I can always walk and talk until I flop. This way . . . here we are. Nice, airy room, you see. Windows. Sun. Everything you could want, I suppose. . . . Have a drink?"

"No," she said.

"Have a drink?" he repeated.

"No," she said.

He poured a drink and gave it to her with ice and siphon. She sipped it, and then sat down.

"Smoke?" he said.

She took a cigarette.

"Rose doesn't smoke," said Willett.

"Is she staying here with you?" asked Jacqueline.

"Not at the moment," answered Willett.

"Ah, you've known her before?"

"There's only one thing that keeps me from knowing her better," said Willett.

"What's the one thing?"

"You."

"Richard, don't talk any more of that stuff."

"Sometimes I'm drunk as a lord, but I'm never drunk as a commoner," he told her. "It's all right. . . . What great thing brought you here?"

"I'm being tailed night and day," she said.

"People laugh at the police," said Willett, "but they're a sensible lot, on the whole. I respect them. They know a dangerous woman when they see one."

"Do you think, honestly, that I'm dangerous?"

"Dangerous as the devil. With equal honesty . . . tell me if you're not?"

"Richard, tell me the truth."

"Well?"

"Are you having an affair with the beautiful Rose Taylor?"

"How do you think I kept her from blackmailing you?" he asked.

"Ah, is that the answer?" She stood up.

"It's only talk," said Willett. "That's why you'll hear from her again, before long."

She was silent.

"I've only plugged the hole in the dam," he explained. "She's apt to start the blackmail dodge again at any time. How close do the police keep to you?"

"They're always around the corner. They're even watching the house. I can't take a ride without seeing someone behind a tree."

"So you came to papa?"

"You hate John, I know. But I'm going to marry him."

"Oh, all right, all right!" said Willett.

He stared at the wall where the last of the day's sun was pouring soft gold. He took another drink.

"I wish you'd put that glass down," she said. "It makes you look ugly, Richard, when you get this much alcohol in you."

"I need liquor when I hear you talk about Telford."

"If he has even a suspicion that I'm connected with the night of the twenty-second, he'll never have a thing to do with me again. However you may hate him, he's the highest-minded and most honorably sensitive man I ever knew. It's the reason

I want to marry him, Richard. Not because I'm so wildly in love with him, but because he's such a rare soul."

"Rare? Damn him, I think he's a murderer."

"Will you help me?"

"To throw off the police?"

"Yes."

"So that you can marry Mr. Telford safely?"

She was silent. He raised the glass to his lips. She took it away from him.

"Don't do that," said Willett.

"You're acting like an ugly little boy," she said, but she gave the glass back. He put it aside on the table.

"Well, I'll help," he said. "They watch you and they watch the house. They wouldn't do both things unless they had a lot of suspicion."

"They may not watch the house when I'm away," she answered.

"Ring up now and find out."

She went to the telephone and got her maid on the wire.

"Alice, have you seen any people hanging around the place?" she asked. "They did? What about . . . ? Did you send it away this morning . . . ? Did you tell them the name of the company? Ah . . . ! Ah . . . ! No, never mind. It's all right. Good-bye."

She hung up.

"The police rang up a little while ago to ask about the yellow dress that I was wearing on the night of the twenty-second," she said. "Alice had sent it away to the cleaners this morning. And now they've asked the name of the company that handles our cleaning! They're going to get that dress and look at it!"

"You're all right. You'll do," said Willett.

"Why do you say that?"

"Only the right ones seem angry when they're frightened."

"Richard, do you know what they'll find on that dress?"

"What?"

"A thin little smudge of green paint near the hem."

115

"What of that?"

"Don't you remember that there was some quite fresh paint on the front door of Uncle David's house? It was green."

"Ah? Why the devil didn't you use some turpentine and take the paint off at home?"

"I was sure that I'd make the smudge worse; and then detectives can tell from the least stain exactly what the thing has been."

"In books they do. You must believe in Santa Claus, also."

He picked up the glass, sniffed it, put it down again. He scowled at her, and she smiled a little in return.

"So I had to send it to the cleaners."

"You might have destroyed it."

"That never works. People try to hide things, but they're always found; and once they're hidden, it makes a mystery. What would Alice have thought if she had seen the dress disappear?"

"It doesn't matter what people are able to think. What matters are the things they're able to do. The police have gone after the dress, have they?"

"Yes. They'll find the paint. They'll put the two things together. I suppose a chemist will be able to tell them that the paint is exactly what was used on Uncle David's door?"

"Where's the cleaners?"

"It's uptown. Baumgarten and Riley. A small place, but good."

"If the police get that dress, what do they know?"

"They know that I had never cared for Uncle David nor he for me. They know that I'm loaded with debts . . . I've been such a fool. They know that I'm almost the sole heir." She took a breath and added, "They know that I'm strong enough to have done everything that was done to Uncle David."

"We've got to get that dress from the cleaners," he said. "You wait here."

"You can't go alone . . . not the way you are now."

"I'm not any way. Whiskey . . . whiskey only makes me a bit impulsive, Jacqueline. So long."

116

When he got to the door she ran after him. He turned around and looked at her.

"Well," he demanded, tersely. His eyes burned into hers.

She said nothing, staring at him, and he went into the hall.

In the closet there he looked until he found a large cap which he tried on. The visor would pull down far over his eyes. He studied the effect in the mirror of the hat rack. Then he left the house.

Three blocks away, he took a taxi bound north.

20

❖

"Yellow Evidence"

On the way, he stopped at a cigar store, found the exact address of Baumgarten and Riley, and rode to within two blocks of it. He walked through the last of the sunset, turned the corner, and entered the block where the shop was located.

The thing looked bad. A group of children were playing at the end of the block. Two or three pedestrians were on the sidewalks. And a car slipped past him, coming up to the curb thirty yards away.

He paused, head down to light a cigarette, for he recognized two of the three figures that climbed out of the car. The slender body and the arrogant air of Campbell were not more distinctive than the squat, fat, bulldog bulk of O'Rourke. With them was a big fellow who took short, neat steps, rising on his toes.

The detectives had brought along one of the proprietors of the shop, of course, to give them access to the place.

The street was a perfect scene for failure, he thought. He took note of the dingy fronts of the houses, leaning shoulder to shoulder, all with porches from which the steps turned abruptly and marched down to the pavement. The roof lines descended in even notches with the slope of the hill, which pitched down at a sharp angle.

The degree of the descent was what gave him his idea. He loitered for a moment, still apparently having trouble with the lighting of his cigarette.

The three were inside the shop, now. Its window gleamed with a pale small light hardly equal to the sunset glow that remained in the sky. Now they were back in the shop; now they must be searching for Jacqueline Barry's dress.

He thought of Telford, and spat into the gutter. Then he stepped to the car which had brought the three to the place. It had not been locked. He reached quickly inside, put the gear lever in neutral, and released the emergency brake. To the steering wheel he gave a last directing touch, and then walked on down the street with a casual step.

He heard the car jounce behind him. It went by, gathering speed. Over some unevenness it swerved and cut across the street at a sharp angle. It accelerated with an uncanny quickness. The slight lurching of the front wheels seemed to indicate a guiding intelligence, steadying at a mark.

Already, down the street, some of the boys at play began to squeal with excitement; then the car struck solidly, against the thick post of a fire hydrant; the automobile lifted up its rear end and crashed, skidded on the pavement, was still, except for small tinkling noises of broken glass, falling.

Willett had gone straight past the entrance to the shop and now paused, turning to stare at the wreck. He had seen, as he passed, three figures running from the interior of Baumgarten and Riley's place. The two detectives came out with the big fellow. They ran on, shouting angrily, toward the smashed car. The big fellow, however, turned abruptly back into his place.

Willett gritted his teeth hard together. Then he followed through the entrance.

If you let the outside of the sole touch the floor first, and then roll the weight carefully forward, a big man can walk quite silently and Willett stepped in that manner.

The shop was in two divisions, a small front office whose shelves were filled with wrapped parcels and beyond a glass partition a much larger interior room where there was an acrid odor in the air, and the peculiar, nauseating smell left by running very hot irons over steaming cloth.

Here, right and left, appeared clothes hanging in long rows from lines, each with a large check attached. Yonder were more clothes piled in assortments.

The big fellow leaned above one of these assortments and pulled out a yellow dress.

From the street outside, the squealing of the crowd had ceased. There was only a rapid chattering to which the distance gave a deeper tone, as though all the children had turned into grown men.

Willett cleared his throat as he tugged his cap down lower over his face. The other turned. It was a fighting face, a big, heavy framework of bone overlaid with layerings of flesh that was a little too soggy. This could not be Baumgarten. It must be Riley. Willett told himself that as he whipped his fist for the jaw.

His blow was straight enough. The instinctive reflex of a trained boxer was what moved the jaw of the big man from the right line. The punch landed a little high. It knocked Riley back on his heels. He grunted and fell forward, his left hand across his face to block, his right hand reaching forward to clinch.

Sometimes a straight punch will drive through that sort of a guard. Sometimes a swinging blow will clip in from the side and do damage. Willett stood on his toes and lifted an uppercut into the face of Riley, knocking his head back.

Still there was Irish fight left in him. His knees were buckling, letting him down as he threw out both arms to drag himself into a clinch. Willett chopped an ugly little right down on the ridge of the jaw. Riley slithered past him, bumped his face on the floor, and lay still.

These damned Irishmen always make trouble. This business had taken too long. As Willett picked up the yellow dress, scuffing it up into a small ball in his hands, he heard voices and footfalls enter the front of the shop.

O'Rourke was saying, "Damned hoodlumism. There oughta be a whip took to the brats, these days; and I'd like to do the taking. The inspector will ride hell out of you when he finds your car is all jimmied up."

"Out of me?" shouted Campbell. "Is it more my fault than yours?"

"A good general," said O'Rourke, obviously speaking inside of quotes, "is responsible for the forces under his command. He doesn't admit the possibility of accident."

"When I hear you jabber like this . . . ," began Campbell. But he broke off. "What's that? Hey? Riley!"

They must have seen the big, prostrate figure through the door that pierced the dividing wall of clouded glass. Willett had stared around him for a moment. There was the back door, but no key to unlock it. He picked up a chair and crashed it through the glass of the rear window.

"After him," shouted Campbell.

"Stop . . . thief!" roared O'Rourke.

They came running. The hole in the window was a vast gap through which two men could have sprung at the same moment, but Willett did not choose to escape in this manner. Instead, he stepped back among the racks of hanging clothes, moving slowly. For at the least touch long waves ran through those diaphanous silks and drapes. He made his way back toward the front of the shop. He could hear the glass of the window being kicked out as the detectives climbed through into the alley.

Then Willett turned out into the street.

There was a knot of twenty people around the ruins of the wrecked automobile. He moved past them. A vast distance opened between him and the next corner, but he forced himself to walk that distance with an unhurried step. Half a block away he caught a taxi, changed from this to another in the West Seventies, and so came home again in the first dark of the night. He paid the driver and went up the steps.

When he unlocked the door, he could hear the voices of Slogger and the girl from the living room. He went in softly. The Slogger was on his feet demonstrating a knockout punch.

121

"When he come in again, I waited and let him have it," said the Slogger, "and he dropped like a . . . hey, hello governor!"

The Slogger went out. Willett took the yellow dress out from under his coat.

"Let's see what's on it?" he asked. He began to run the hem through his fingers.

"What happened?" asked Jacqueline Barry.

"I got it, all right," he said. "Here . . . looks like a grass stain, but it's paint, all right. I'm glad we have this, Jacqueline."

"How did you manage to find it?" she asked.

"I had some help on the finding," he told her. "What's going to be done with it? Burn it? Is it cool enough to rate a fire on the hearth, this evening?"

He opened the window. River damp blew in with the evening wind.

Jacqueline shivered.

"Plenty cold enough," he decided.

He tore a sheet from a newspaper, crumpled it, lighted it. A fire was already laid and he stuffed the sheet of newspaper under the kindling. The flame shot down under the wood, twinkled, shrank. Dense white smoke began to rise, began to lip over the edge of the fireplace and ripple up like sea fog across the mantelpiece and the mirror above it.

The girl was silent, watching, alert. When he saw her face in the mirror, the smoke made it dimmer than an old memory.

"We burn the fire," said he, "and we burn the dress in it. Cloth always leaves a rank odor in the air. And that's bad. Mighty bad. . . . How can we get around that?"

He looked at Jacqueline. She was thoughtful, but she had no solution to offer. Compared with Rose Taylor, she was almost plain; but Rose Taylor was a worthless unreality by another comparison.

He pulled the upholstery off one of the chairs—the loose covering of linen print that exposed beneath it a plain, strong, blue cloth.

"This ought to do," said Willett.

The flame had broken upward through the kindling, by this

time. Handfuls of fire exploded up the chimney, sucking the white smoke with it. The kindling caught, crackling, and, as the flame began to roar, he piled the dress and the linen cover together on the fire. He held it up so that the unsmothered fire could get its teeth into the new food more easily. The cloth caught. He dropped the folds of it and watched the yellow flames shooting into the chimney.

"This chair was standing too close to the fire," he explained, "and a jump of the flames caught it. Before I knew, it was in a blaze. I had to snatch it off. Bad moment. You can understand what might have happened if I hadn't noticed just in time?" He smiled down at her.

Jacqueline laughed, very softly.

"You'd better go," he said. "You were seen coming here, and the news might spread. I ought not to have let you wait here until I got back. I could have telephoned the news to you."

"Only Rose Taylor knows that I'm here," she said.

"What about the police who were shadowing you?"

"I led them a crazy chase and drove through three traffic lights on the way. They couldn't have followed me. I left my car two blocks from here."

"Good girl," said Willett. "But you'd better go, now."

"I don't want to go," she answered. "I want to find out just what happened. There at the dry cleaners, I mean."

"It was a sort of a tangle, that's all," answered Willett. "I'd rather talk about something else."

"But how did you get into the place?" she asked.

"I was thinking," said Willett, "that if you were not about to have five millions in the old purse, I might not be so tiptoes about you."

"It isn't the money," she answered. "It's John. If he wants me, you'd be interested in spiting him."

"Is that it?" asked Willett. "Have another drink."

"No. You'd better not, either."

He looked down the back of his knuckles. They felt a bit sore, but there were no obvious marks. Then he lifted his old glass. The whiskey was warmish, but that made it all the better.

"This Telford business is the bunk," said Willett.

"I don't think it is," she answered.

"Isn't it damned compromising for you to be here . . . at night . . . all that sort of thing?"

"I suppose it is. But I want to hear what happened to you. Something exciting happened. I could tell by the happy, childish look of you when you came back."

"If you stay here, I'm going to talk about you and me."

"I'll have to go then," said Jacqueline.

"Suppose we step out for some dinner?"

"That wouldn't be good. If word came back to John that I was going about with you, he'd be worried."

"Oh, damn John!"

"Talking isn't much good, is it?" said the girl. "But one of these days, suppose that I have a chance to let you know how I appreciate what you've done for me, Richard?"

He looked at her a long moment.

"Some day I'll be broke and come to you for a grubstake, I suppose," said Willett. "Then money will talk. Money is about the only thing that does, eh?"

"You know something, Richard?"

"Sometimes."

"You're not half as hard as you pretend."

"No? No. I'm not hard at all."

"The Slogger has been telling me a few things."

"He has to talk, the half-wit."

The doorbell rang.

"I wish you weren't here," he said.

"I wouldn't be any other place," she answered.

The Slogger opened the door a crack.

"Coupla detectives. O'Rourke and Campbell names," he said.

"Wait a minute," said Willett.

"Is there a back way out?" she asked. "No, I wouldn't do that. I'll go out past them. I won't sneak."

"You'd better be wise and sneak," said Willett.

"I won't do it," she answered. "Good-bye, Richard."

He went to the front door with her and showed her out. She spoke to the two detectives cheerfully and went straight on down the steps.

Campbell said, "If I'd known you were leaving, I'd of brought your car up from around the corner."

She turned on the sidewalk and looked back, silently, at Campbell; then she walked up the street with a good, free, swinging step.

21

❖

"Murderer's Accomplice"

Willett took the pair into the library. He did not offer drinks, although O'Rourke looked hungrily at the loaded tray.

"Fire on a summer night?" asked Campbell.

"River damp in the air," said Willett.

Campbell went to the fire. He picked up the poker and thrust it into a mass of material that had lumped at one side of the blaze. As the air got into the center of the lump, it burned with a sudden brightness. Campbell brought it out onto the hearth at the end of the poker.

"Burning some of the upholstery, Willett?" he asked.

"Left the chair too near and the stuff caught fire," said Willett.

Campbell poked into the fire again. He slipped the iron through the ashes. Then he straightened with a sigh.

"Let me see your right hand," he said.

"Have you got a search warrant?" asked Willett, smiling. But he held out his hand.

"Lookit, Pat," commented Campbell.

O'Rourke came and stared.

"Not much sign," he said. "Lemme see the left."

"Measuring me for gloves?" asked Willett.

"He done the most with the left. Look!" said O'Rourke. "Go and get Riley, Angus."

The Scotchman went outside.

"Getting thicker and thicker, ain't it?" asked O'Rourke. He grinned at Willett.

126

"I can't help taking pity when I see that face of yours," said Willett. "Have a drink?"

"I need one," answered O'Rourke.

He took a big one and lighted one of his cigars. "Ain't you playing it sort of fast and narrow, brother?"

"How?" asked Willett.

"I'm with you, big boy. Anybody with a fin as hard as you, that can flick over a bird like Riley and not bark the skin off his knuckles, certainly has my support. But why do you do it? What's the girl to you?"

"Of course I don't know what you're talking about," said Willett.

"Of course you don't," said O'Rourke.

Campbell came back with Riley. He had a lump on one side of his face. His mouth was swollen.

"Take a look at Mr. Willett," said Campbell. "Does he look familiar to you?"

"You mean," said Riley, "was this the guy that slammed me?"

He walked up until he was only a step from Willett and measured him with a fighting eye.

"The mug that put the grease under me was two inches taller and thirty pounds more than Mr. Willett," said Riley.

"What about the face?"

"The bird that slammed me had a Jack Dempsey look," said Riley.

"That's all you want to say?" asked O'Rourke.

"That's all."

"You can go, then," answered O'Rourke. "Take him out, Angus."

Campbell took the man away. "That's the sort of luck a detective plays in," said O'Rourke. "There's no reason that Riley shouldn't have identified you, except that you hit the same time as he laid eyes on you. He says it was a square-shooter that give him a word and a chance to turn around and put up his props before he was socked. That made a big hit with Riley. He's an amateur boxer, Mr. Willett. He says that

127

nobody but a pro could have put him to sleep with three little taps, like you did."

"This all sounds interesting," said Willett. "Who's been working up a reputation for me, Sergeant?"

"You won't talk, eh? Not even a little bit? Not even among friends?" said O'Rourke, sadly. "People don't trust a cop. That's one of the troubles with this work. People don't trust us."

The telephone rang and Willett went to it.

"Sergeants Campbell and O'Rourke there?" asked a voice.

"Somebody wants you two," said Willett.

Campbell took the receiver. "Campbell speaking."

"Bares reporting," said a voice. "I tailed Rose Taylor to a telephone booth. She went from there down to her house. She done herself into a black dress and come out again. She went uptown to 85th Street and into a German restaurant there. I hung around. After a while, in comes John Telford. He's in there talking to her now."

"Cut in," urged Campbell. "Find out what they're talking about."

"That's hard to do. She's as tricky as a cat on the watch."

"Don't tell me it's hard to do. Do it!"

Campbell hung up.

"I guess we won't bother Mr. Willett any more," he said.

O'Rourke said, "I wish you were on our side, Mr. Willett.

"Well, maybe I am," answered Willett.

When they got out on the street, O'Rourke mopped his face. He went to his car with Campbell, in silence. Then he waved a hand. From the darkness between two stairways across the street, a figure came out and hurried to them.

"Listen, Chalmers," said Campbell. "How long was Miss Barry in that place?"

"Since along early in the evening."

"All the time in there?"

"Yes."

"She didn't come out once, for instance?"

"Not unless she sneaked out a back way."

"And Willett . . . you told me about him leaving. How did he come back? In a rush?"

"Stepping easy," said Chalmers.

O'Rourke and Campbell drove off.

"You heard that," said Campbell. "Stepping easy. Now here's the hell of working for the law. We know just what happened. Jacqueline Barry found out we were on the trail of her dress. She runs to Willett for help, and he helps her. He burgles the shop, gets the dress, takes it back to his place, and lets her see him burn it. We know all that; we oughta be able to slam him in the cooler for a coupla years. But we can't. Why? Because this is America, the home of the free and the land of the brave. Free? Free be damned! What chance has an officer of the law in this part of the world? No chance at all. You gotta have a signed statement by five witnesses, eyewitnesses; and then a handwriting expert comes along and puts the signatures in the wash. But Willett killed Barry. That's what I'll prove in the long run. And maybe Jacqueline Barry gave him a hand."

"How come?" demanded O'Rourke.

"Otherwise, why does she run to him for help?"

"Ah, shut up," said O'Rourke. "Leave me think. The Scotch of your way of talkin' puts smoke in my brain. Where do we go from here is the next thing?"

"Green paint. The smell of the fresh paint on the front door of the Barry house. That's what I keep thinkin' about," said Campbell.

"Sure you do," said O'Rourke. "That's what you *would* think about. What about finding the report of the accountant on Morrison's ledger?"

"I know," said Campbell. "We might get that and put the screws on Morrison again. How does he take jail?"

"He'll be out on bail tomorrow, and he knows it. So his face is filling out again."

"Did he kill Pollok?" asked Campbell.

"It's the sort of a job that a sneak like Morrison might do. And Pollok knew Rose Taylor. Somehow the two jobs have got to tie in. Pollok killed Barry."

"Never in your life," said Campbell.

"No? And why not?"

"Pollok was a lad that had a gun and knew how to use it. If he killed Barry . . . why?"

"Barry always carried several thousand dollars around on him."

"Too much circumstantial evidence against you," said Campbell. "Pollok, a gunman, breaks in on Barry, kills him, takes his money. But look at it this way; Pollok is the chum of Rose Taylor, who is the secretary of Morrison, who is the partner of Barry. Makes a chain, don't it? I say, if Barry was killed by Pollok, Morrison had his hand in it. Morrison says to his secretary: 'I wish to God that somebody would put Barry out of the way.' Sweet little Rose says: 'Why not?' and she goes to Pollok. Does that sound natural? Barry is dead, but now Pollok puts pressure on Morrison for more money. Morrison decides to do in Pollok. There you get the whole circle."

"Deduction!" said O'Rourke. "I don't give a damn for a whole bale of deductions, printed small on legal tender. Not a damn. Facts are what count. Anybody can think anything into a straight line. But it takes more'n talk to put a crook in the electric chair. Telford's the man, Angus. Telford . . . maybe with a lift from Morrison. We'll go take a talk with that accountant."

22

❖

"A Coward Collapses"

Big Jeffrey Morrison was aware of a horrible uncertainty of body and mind. His lips felt thick and numb, as though he had been drinking too much for many days. His hands were soft. There was no strength in them.

He said, "You boys have made your play. My lawyer tells me that this all has been a damned outrage, and I've a mind to make you pay for it. A damned good mind . . . ! Now what you want to talk to me about? I'm not in your dirty jail, now. You can remember that!"

"You're out for a while. Just for a while," said Angus Campbell. "O'Rourke, how long would you say that he'd stay out?"

O'Rourke remained at the window, looking at lower Manhattan's towers with unseeing eyes.

"You talk to that mug. I don't want to talk to him," said O'Rourke.

Campbell opened a large briefcase and took out a ledger.

"You know this?" he asked.

"I know it was stolen out of my office . . . out of the safe in my office. If that's not burglary, what is? You can go to jail for this, Sergeant Campbell."

The sergeant moistened his thin lips. The only part of his face that ever changed color was his ears. Now they turned to a flaming crimson.

He said, "Mr. Morrison, I've picked pockets, and tapped people on the head, and third-degreed 'em with a length of rubber hose, and jimmied windows by night, and lied my way all around the clock. I had your ledger stolen. And I had a first-class public accountant go over the book. You can have it back. Here it is. I don't need it anymore. I've got his signed statement in my pocket. In four years you stole over a hundred thousand dollars from your firm of Barry and Morrison."

Morrison closed his eyes. There was an optician who said that if a man wanted to rest the eyes and the brain the thing to do was to close the lids and then think of black velvet. Morrison tried to think about black velvet but all he could see were headlines in a great daily paper, and the faces of the men at his club.

"When you owed Barry a hundred thousand dollars, all at once Barry died. And that was too bad, wasn't it?" asked Campbell.

O'Rourke drew a cuspidor nearer with his foot and spat into it. Morrison looked at O'Rourke. The back of the fat detective spoke more eloquently than words.

"The fact is, gentlemen . . . , said Morrison. He cleared his throat. This was not a meeting of a board of directors, after all. "Campbell," he said, "there's been a terrible mistake."

"Yeah. Sure, sure!" said Campbell. "It was terrible for Barry."

"To assist the law," said Morrison, "anything that I could do. . . ."

"Before Barry died . . . when was the last time you saw him?"

"I? I don't remember."

"Start in remembering or you go back to jail for embezzlement."

"I think it was the day before."

"The twenty-first?"

"Yes. That would be it."

"Where did you meet him?"

"Let me see. Ah, yes. It was in my offices."

"His offices, too, weren't they?"

"Naturally."

"How often did Barry come down to those same offices?"

"Not often. The whole burden of the business was left to me."

"All Barry did was to fork over the hard cash, eh?" asked Campbell.

"The experience, the brain, the contacts, all the hard work and the pull . . . and Barry, of course, supplied some of the capital."

"I know," said Campbell. "Tell me something . . . what did you talk about that day, the twenty-first, in your office?"

"Affairs in general," said Morrison. "There was plenty to talk about. He kept so far away from the business concerns of our firm. He left everything. . . ."

"Did he ever look into this ledger?"

"Ledger? Why, I don't think so."

"Morrison, you're walking the edge of a cliff that's a mile high. Will you tell me the truth?"

"I don't understand what. . . ."

"Did you keep this ledger always in the safe?"

"Yes, I think. . . ."

"I can find out, easily enough," said Campbell. "I can find out just where it usually was. Did you keep it always in the safe?"

"Not that I recall," said Morrison.

"You're sweating like a pig, already," said Campbell. "What the hell kind of a man are you, anyway? If you wanta lie, can't you keep your face to yourself? You didn't keep the ledger in the safe, usually, then?"

"No," said Morrison.

With a handkerchief he wiped his face. The heat struck through the cloth. He thought about apoplexy. If he fell dead, these two fellows would have some explaining to do to the law!

"When did you put it in the safe?"

"After talking . . . ," said Morrison, and stuck there, staring.

"After talking with Barry, that day?"

The truth uttered itself slowly, without volition, out of the throat of Jeffrey Morrison.

"Yes, after talking with Barry, I put it. . . ."

"Into the safe, eh?"

"Yes."

"Barry didn't see it before you put it into the safe?"

"I think not. No."

"That day, he came to ask some questions about business and business profits, eh?"

"Yes," said Morrison.

"Go on and talk. Do I have to use jail to blast the truth out of you?"

"He came," said Morrison. "He had a mean way about him of looking and sneering when he talked. He was sneering a good deal that day. He didn't understand that a business needs time to develop and that early profits often don't appear to. . . ." He hesitated, mopped his brow again.

"The hundred thousand you stole you put back into the business, eh?"

"In indirect ways. . . ."

"Like the price of a pretty stenographer, eh?"

"Why . . . ah . . . Miss Taylor. . . ."

"Barry was on your trail," said Campbell. "That was why you went out to his house on the evening of the twenty-second?"

"Yes."

"That was why you pulled a gun?"

"Yes," groaned Morrison. "I thought . . . I thought. . . ."

"You made your last bluff and, when it wouldn't work, you left the finishing of Barry to another man, eh?" asked Campbell.

"No!" shouted Morrison.

"You lie, you dog," said Campbell, calmly.

Morrison sank back into his chair. Courtesy is a beautiful thing. He wondered why there should be so much discourtesy in this world of ours. He looked at the back of O'Rourke. It was a fat but a savage back. It fenced away the last hope in the world.

"When you left the house of Barry, where did you go?"

134

"I drove down the road. Telford's house was near."

"Ah," said O'Rourke. He turned about from the window. "What did you want to see Lord John Telford about?"

"He was Barry's lawyer."

"How much business did you do with him?" asked O'Rourke.

"Why, I saw him from time to time. Naturally I saw him."

"He handled this contracting business for Barry?"

"He handled Mr. Barry's affairs in a general way."

"Haven't we heard that it was through Telford that you got Barry into your hands?"

"It's true that we met through John Telford."

"And Telford looked over the books and took care. . . ."

"He only took a general supervision. Telford is a young man, but he's very busy."

O'Rourke said, "Isn't it true that John Telford is as big a crook as you are?"

"Telford? Crook?" said Morrison. He turned pale. "My God, of course not!"

"He didn't fake an agreement with you and split the profits that you stole from Barry?" shouted O'Rourke, furiously.

"No, no! I swear to God. . . ."

"Shut up!" commanded O'Rourke.

Campbell turned his head, slowly, and looked at O'Rourke. Campbell's cheeks were wrinkling. That was his nearest approach to a smile. His face was unschooled in the production of pleasant expressions. He didn't need them and therefore he seldom used them.

"What did you talk to Telford about?" demanded O'Rourke.

"I told him that Barry was excited. I hoped that Barry wouldn't do anything foolish. That was about all."

"You didn't say *why* Barry might be apt to do something foolish?"

"I said . . . you know . . . in any partnership, misunderstandings . . . I tried to give Mr. Telford the impression that everything would be all right if he could make Mr. Barry a little

135

more patient. That was about what we talked of."

"That was when?"

"Along in the twilight of the day."

"Where did you see Telford?"

"At his house."

"I know that. But where in his house?"

"I just stepped into his study."

"It was raining then, or not?"

"No, the rain hadn't begun."

"You're sure?"

"Yes. Sure."

"Where were you standing when Sid Pollok was shot through the head?" snapped O'Rourke.

Morrison gasped. His eyes rolled. He thrust himself half out of his chair with arms that trembled under the weight of his fat bulk. And then he collapsed again, his chin on his breast. His flesh quivered. O'Rourke went over and stooped and stared into his face.

"What a fat, soggy coward you are!" said O'Rourke.

23

❖

"Murderer's Knock"

Afterwards O'Rourke said, "Go on and deduce something, Angus. It's a hell of a long time since you deduced
anything. Maybe you ain't been reading books about great detectives, lately."

"There's some," said Campbell, "that's ignorant and are
wanting to do something about it; there's some that are ignorant and are ashamed of it even if they don't try to learn; but
there's some that lie down and wallow in their ignorance, like
swine in the mud!"

"That sounds to me almost like a Bible lesson," said
O'Rourke. "What are you deducin', though?"

"I'm thinking about green paint," said Campbell.

"We'll go look at it, then," answered O'Rourke.

THE SUN WAS SLANTED with burning brilliance against the front
of the Barry house when they reached the place. Matilda
Grunsky, with her hair twisted into a knot on the top of her
head, opened the door to them. Her pale little eyes grew wide
at the sight of them.

"We want to look around a little, that's all," said O'Rourke.
"By the way, when was this front door painted last?"

"It was painted the morning of the last day," said Matilda
Grunsky.

"Kind of ghostly, ain't it, staying on here since Barry died?"

"No, sir, not for me," said Matilda Grunsky. "There's not
much work to do when I'm just caretaking. But I come over

137

here and spend a spell of time every day. Because it does me good."

"How does it do you good?" asked O'Rourke.

"The silence. Sometimes, without knowing, my nerves get all tautened up. I get nervous. I begin to hold my breath. I get scared and kind of a little sick. And then all at once I remember that I'll never have to hear his voice again, and that makes me feel pretty good. That's why I come over here and spend quite a spell, every day."

"You didn't like him," nodded O'Rourke.

"Only the devil could of liked him," said Matilda.

"Mean to work for?"

"Sometimes he'd go a week and never speak. I used to write out the menu every day for the following day. He'd write what he wanted changed. If I suggested an omelet, he'd write: 'Not like the last one.' Once I asked him how he wanted the roast cooked. He said: 'With intelligence.' I meant, with brown potatoes or something. He had that way with his tongue. He thought everybody was a fool, and that every fool was a bad fool. God forgive me, but I'm glad he's dead!"

She backed into the hall.

"Will you gentlemen come in?" she asked.

"Have you got a reading glass on you?" asked Campbell.

"For what?"

"I want to look at the paint on this door," said Campbell.

"And you mean to say that you haven't got a microscope in your pocket?" demanded O'Rourke.

"No. Sure I haven't. How would I have one?"

"Every detective that I ever read about," said O'Rourke, "always had pockets as big as satchels. They'd got jointed jimmies for opening windows, and a pair of guns, and a knife with a magnetized blade, and a screwdriver, and a pocket torch, and a sort of universal periscope with a telescope eye that can both see and listen to a fly walking a mile away; and I'm not talking about the cloth soles they have for their shoes, or the special lenses that they keep for their monocles; but sure every one of them would never be seen on the street without a microscope

138

or two. What's your reading been profiting you, Sergeant Campbell? Just words without no meaning? Ain't you been following Baron von Osling, the great Hungarian goulash that reads lips and minds like nothing at all? The Baron, he never steps outside his house without a whole kit of burglar tools worked into the seams of his clothes. And they never make him weigh a pound heavier and they never make a rattle or a clink. But you coming here and asking me have I got a reading glass is what beats me. Sure I haven't got a reading glass. I was sure that a great detective like Campbell, that deduces and everything, would have a whole automobile kit of everything we could want."

Campbell looked through a long moment at O'Rourke. The dispassionate disgust rounded the projecting orbs of his eyeballs. Still looking at O'Rourke, he said, "Miss Grunsky, would you bring me a water bottle if you got one made of smooth glass, not all carved up? A water bottle, filled with water?"

She was glad to be useful, she said as she went off, and she came back to them in a moment with a round-bellied carafe in her hand. The sunlight set a fire of melting diamonds inside the water.

Campbell, in the meantime, had dusted the face of the door carefully. Now he took the water bottle and moved it slowly over the face of the wood, covering the central section.

"Don't be afraid, Matilda," said O'Rourke. "And don't be surprised. You get a good book detective outside of the print and he's apt to do a lot of things. There's Campbell, now, offering a drink to some green paint. Kind of queer, you'd say, but not . . . Campbell is only getting ready to deduce. You remember Sherlock Holmes? He'd take morphine and things to steady himself before he begun to deduce. But Campbell, here, takes a look at green paint through a water bottle."

"Shut up," said Campbell, "and look here for yourself. Let the water steady in the bottle and then look at the green paint, right in here."

He pointed out the place. O'Rourke, taking the bottle, held

it up before the paint and stared through. He was grinning a little. A slight wavering of the liquid inside the glass cast over the door thin films of shadow that floated up and down, steadied, and enabled him to look through with ease at the considerably magnified surface of the paint.

"See anything?" asked Campbell.

"No. Nothing but paint and the grain of the wood under it. Yes, and a couple of nail heads."

"You'll see something else . . . in here."

O'Rourke looked again, for a long time, until his arms ached from holding up the water bottle.

"Here!" said Campbell. "Try it this way."

He picked up some dust and blew it carefully off the tips of his fingers onto a portion of the door. "That brings it out?" asked Campbell.

"Three little hollows in the paint," said O'Rourke. "What of it? Maybe a carpenter's hammer stuttered on the wood."

"Those dents are in the paint, only," answered Campbell.

"Well, suppose they are; what of it?"

O'Rourke stood back. Campbell took the water bottle and gave it back to Matilda Grunsky.

"You see those dents, though?" said Campbell.

"Yeah, I'm not blind."

"I'm going to make a tracing of 'em and put the tracing beside the dents. Then you tell me if they're any different from the originals. Sit down over there and smoke a cigar . . . or chew your tongue and be damned. Why do I have to be hitched to an Irish fathead when there's real work to do? What would the inspector say if you and me could be *seen* working on a case together?" said Campbell.

"He'd cut 'deduction' out of the police brain," said O'Rourke.

Campbell took a thin sheet of paper out of a notebook and with it, carefully and painfully, he produced with his pencil a faint outline and then a darker shading of the three indentations.

"Come look," he said. "Right in here. . . . And blow the

stink of that cigar smoke the other way, will you . . . ? Do those look like the real thing?"

"They're the same size and distance apart. Yeah, they're the same," said O'Rourke. "Is the world gonna break in two, now?"

"Suppose that you came here on the night of the twenty-second," said Campbell. "You had yourself keyed up to anything as far as murder. You'd known this place back to the days when there was no electricity for lights . . . and the bell on the door. You might have forgotten the bell and you might have rapped, mightn't you?"

"Ah?" said O'Rourke. He stared at Campbell.

"Suppose the paint had been put on that same day; it might have kept a little impression of the knocks, mightn't it? Dents like these?"

"I suppose so."

"Everybody's got a different way of knocking at a door," remarked Campbell. "Some of 'em knock with the front of the knuckles and some with the back. Different ways for different places, too. Suppose that you step out and come to a door where there's somebody that you don't know. You give two raps, one the same loudness as the other. Suppose it's a friend, you give three or four knocks to show you're there. Everybody would hit the door in a different way, too. I mean, one would put all the three raps in about the same place. One would have two together and one lower down. It's a thing a man don't think about, and so he always would do it in the same way. Is that lodged in your thick Irish skull?"

"Angus," said O'Rourke, "I feel like Columbus or some-body. Maybe I've discovered an idea in your head."

"I'm going to get to the next village and find some quick-drying green paint," said Campbell. "In an hour I'll have this door painted. By night, it'll be dry as the paint was the night of the twenty-second when these raps were given to the door. You're going back to New York. Round up everybody. Willett, first. Willett's the man. He hadn't been here for five years and the electricity had been put in since he was last at the

141

house. He came . . . he gave this knock . . . and then he murdered David Barry. But get the rest, too. Everybody that figures. Get Telford, Rose Taylor, Morrison, Jacqueline Barry. See that they all show up here one after another, at intervals, so that no two come in at the same time."

"You want Rose Taylor, too?" said O'Rourke. "She hasn't the strength to handle even a skinny runt like Barry the way he was handled . . . if murder's the answer. How do we know it wasn't suicide and then a plant?"

Campbell's face contorted.

"Why the hell talk about that?" he demanded. "You go and do what I say."

And, of course, O'Rourke obeyed orders without further argument. He seemed depressed.

24

❖

"Telford Talks"

They gathered in a small group before the Barry house. Willett, Telford, Jacqueline Barry. O'Rourke held them there.

"This is important," said O'Rourke, "and we're asking you to go in one by one, please. Miss Barry, you go now, if you don't mind."

She left them and went with a quick step toward the house.

"It seems a little queer," said Telford, "that we should have to go through this nonsense."

"I'll tell you what, Mr. Telford," said the Irishman, "whenever a Scotchman gets an idea, which isn't often, it's pretty sure to be an idea that's worthwhile. This is Campbell's scheme."

He turned to watch Jacqueline Barry at the door of the house. They could hear, thin as a noise from another world, the sound of the bell ringing inside the house. O'Rourke said, "That's good!"

"What's good?" asked Telford.

"Oh, nothing," answered O'Rourke. "Nice night, ain't it? Softish, sort of. I gotta be out in all sorts of weather, the sort of work I do, and I get so's I hate the face of the sky at night. I gotta think of so many winter times when I been out froze in my tracks and tryin' to keep my brain awake. But now's I get older I have a different way of living. I leave winter to itself and summer to itself. But it's a funny thing that the same stars that freeze the hell out of you in winter are the ones that makes the daisies on a summer night."

"That's poetic, O'Rourke," said Telford.

143

"Yeah, and ain't it?" murmured O'Rourke. "But it's not poetry that's gonna take place inside the Barry house tonight."

"A fellow like you," said Telford, "should find a better kind of work than being a detective. That's not what you want to be."

"No," said O'Rourke, "and when I get a chance, I'm gonna get me a little place in the country and have some cows. I'm gonna milk those cows and hang pictures inside the house of Pat O'Rourke carryin' pails of milk. And I'm gonna have a dog like I had when I was a kid. The kids have all the fun. The kids and old folks. But here in the middle swim a man has to take care of his wife when she's turned into a mug, and his brats when they're all arms and legs and bellies and beginning to pay him back in sass for the money he's spent on 'em. Mr. Telford, will you go in now . . . ? No, I guess it's Mr. Willett's turn. Step in, Mr. Willett?"

Willett went to the front door. The air was wonderfully still. A marvelously small odor of fresh paint reached them as they watched. They heard the small, thin ring of the bell again.

"Good again," said O'Rourke.

"What's good about it?" asked Telford.

"Ever take a look at the straight back of Willett and wonder if he's not a better man than you think him to be?" asked O'Rourke.

"He's been in my mind every day since I first met him," said Telford, "and I've always hated the thought of him."

"What happened the first day you met?"

"At school? We had a fight. You see him a big chunk of a man, now. But he was a strip of wire, then. Just a strip of wire. Nothing more. I was a lot taller and heavier. I was too heavy to have picked on him, but he was new at the school and he wanted to fight his way into place, so he picked out the biggest . . . It wasn't a fight. It was a slaughter. I knocked him down till his face was red from the chin up. His eyebrows were painted red. So was the forward shag of hair that dropped over his forehead. I asked him to give up. He wouldn't. Finally I slipped and he hit me at the same time. He dropped on me and got a stranglehold. Both arms locked around my neck. The other boys tried to pull him off. He wouldn't let go. They had to beat him off me. They had to kick him off. His arm was hooked around my throat, so that I still can remember it. The way the air wouldn't come when I bit at it. The way the things around me turned black with red streaks spinning across the blackness. They got him off in time. But I never forgot. I was ten seconds from being strangled, I suppose. And ever since I've remembered. I saw the murder in him, that day. It made me sick at the stomach, and then it made me hate him."

"That's a good yarn," said O'Rourke. "When he got bigger, ever fight him again?"

"Once, with gloves. We fought ourselves ragged. It was a draw."

"The point is that you two never have had it out," said O'Rourke. "There's nothing so good for a man as having it out with the other fellow. It kind of washes the head clean and clear again. I remember Jimmy Murphy. We fought seven times. He lived on my block. The last time, we wound up both sitting in the gutter looking at each other. And we began to laugh. We been good friends ever since. Maybe the same thing will happen between you and Willett."

"Maybe," said Telford, and added no more, though O'Rourke waited.

"Will you go in now, Mr. Telford?"

"Certainly," said Telford, and walked to the door. He went with a quick, hurried step, his head thrusting forward a little. When he came to the door, he rapped on it. O'Rourke heard the three taps distinctly—and afterwards there was the ring of the bell.

O'Rourke took a deep breath. He ran his fingers gingerly across his throat.

The door swung open on the brightness of the hallway and Sergeant Campbell waiting inside. Then O'Rourke hastened.

When he was in the hallway, Telford already was entering the living room, out of which came a hum of voices. Campbell remained in the hall.

145

"Well?" said O'Rourke.

Campbell gave him a black look and walked past him. He took from his vest pocket a small lens and with it searched the surface of the paint. At last he found what he wanted and put it beside his tracing of the older indentations.

"I counted them. Three knocks," said O'Rourke. "It's Telford that came here the night of the twenty-second and rapped at the door. Mr. Murderer Telford, Campbell! You've set your own trap and caught your own fish, Angus. I knew, but you had to do the proving."

Campbell folded the paper and put it back inside his notebook.

"It was Telford that rapped the night of the twenty-second," he admitted, "but . . ."

"But what?"

"Never mind."

"He went back into the house with O'Rourke after him. "Go careful," said O'Rourke. "If you jam Telford into a tight spot, he's going to make trouble or I'm a liar."

"Every Irishman was born a liar," said Campbell. "You can't help what you are."

He led on into the living room.

They were making a smooth moment of it, all chatting easily together. They seemed quite natural. Telford was talking with Rose Taylor. Willett, Jacqueline, and Morrison made the other group.

"Look at the two of 'em in the same room," said O'Rourke. "Rose Taylor looked like a world-beater when she was by herself. But she's a selling platter compared with a champion like the Barry gal."

"Damn the looks of them," said Campbell. "Maybe one of them done the murder the night of the twenty-second right here in this room."

And he glanced up toward the balcony from which the body of David Barry once had dangled, turning slowly at the end of its rope.

146

They had arranged beforehand how the conversation should go. O'Rourke took the lead.

He said, "All of you who were inside this room the night of the twenty-second, lift the right hand."

Morrison lifted his hand.

"None of the rest of you came here?" asked O'Rourke.

There was no answer.

Campbell broke in. "All innocent. Look at their faces and you can see that they're innocent . . . damned innocent. Come on, now. What you won't say, we're gonna drag out of you. You can't beat us. We know."

"All away . . . none of you here, eh?" asked Campbell. "Well, go on, O'Rourke."

"You came here the night of the twenty-second," said O'Rourke. "I'm looking at you, Mr. Telford."

Telford said nothing.

"You came here and knocked at the front door," said O'Rourke. "You knocked three times. There was fresh paint on the door. And today that paint was freshened again. You got a little excited this evening, standing out there talking with me. Weren't you a little excited the night of the twenty-second, when you came here and rapped three times . . . on some fairly soft paint?"

Telford shrugged his shoulders.

"That's absolutely absurd," said Jacqueline Barry.

Telford turned to her.

"Thank you, Jacqueline," he said. "But the fact is that I *was* here."

"That's that!" snapped O'Rourke. "Sometimes it's harder than this to make a man talk. Glad to have it out of you, Telford. With a few witnesses around. Suppose you come out with the truth . . . the rest of it. *Why* were you here?"

"The fact is," said Telford, "that it was a rather intimate conversation."

"Don't you figger," said O'Rourke, "that this is a kind of an intimate bunch of people that we've got together? Only one murder to go around and five people to serve with it. What were you doing here the night of the twenty-second?"

"I'm sorry about this, Jacqueline," said Telford.

"Be perfectly open, John," she said.

She was not nervous, Willett thought.

"Well," said Telford, "the truth is that Barry was making some trouble about my marriage with his niece . . . his cousin, really. That was the only actual relationship. And that night I came here to persuade him, if I could, that it would be better to let us have the ceremony performed right away. He objected. He had some queer freaks of mind and fancy. That night he chose to feel that Miss Barry had piled up too many debts and that she would have to do penance for a time. I couldn't budge him. He was adamant. At last I found myself losing my temper. It was no use. I left and went home in the rain. The next morning, when I heard about the tragedy, of course I wanted to cover up the fact that I had been here. People would draw too many obvious conclusions when they saw how much I stood to gain by that death. Gain through a marriage with Miss Barry, you understand. That's all there is to it. I should have told you all this before, Sergeant. It was on the tip of my tongue a good many times."

25

❖

"Rose Taylor Talks"

This speech from Telford made O'Rourke and Campbell glance at one another, Campbell with a faint smile of triumph, O'Rourke with an equally faint shrug of the shoulders.

O'Rourke said suddenly, "I suppose Mr. Telford is telling the truth. I suppose everyone will tell the truth. But I suppose you may as well know that if Barry was murdered, the murderer is probably in this room now. We want some more information. Miss Taylor! Suppose you tell us what you did, exactly, on the evening and the night of the twenty-second?"

She waited for a moment. Attention had time to focus on her before she said, looking at the floor: "That afternoon at his office Mr. Morrison seemed quite nervous."

There was a rustling noise. Morrison had readjusted himself in his chair and was staring at the girl. She kept looking at the floor.

Rose Taylor went on, "Mr. Morrison was so nervous that I noticed it."

"How did he show the nerves?" asked Campbell.

"He would start to dictate a letter and then forget what he was saying."

"Rose!" burst out Morrison.

She looked at Morrison without her smile. She sighed.

Campbell said, softly, "You keep your mouth shut while she's talking. Afterwards, you'll have plenty of chance to yap."

Morrison settled back in his chair. He gripped his hands hard together. In his face was a staring incredulity.

149

"Mr. Morrison was so upset," said Rose Taylor, "that I began to think about it, and wonder a little. We left the office at the same time. I went down in the elevator with Mr. Morrison and said good evening to him on the sidewalk. He hurried away to his car. I went around the corner where. . . ."

She made a slight pause.

"It's all right," said O'Rourke. "We're friendly. Go right ahead and spill the beans."

"Well," said Rose, blushing. "Sidney Pollok was waiting for me in his car, around the corner, you see. And when I got in I told him how extremely nervous Mr. Morrison had been, and Mr. Pollok thought perhaps it would be better to see where Mr. Morrison went and what he did. Mr. Morrison was so *very* nervous."

"Ha!" said Morrison.

"Will you shut up?" snarled Campbell, making a fist of his right hand.

The girl went on, "So we followed Mr. Morrison. He went two or three places. He was a little time at his club. Then he drove out of the city into the country. We just kept him in sight, you know, and finally we saw him turn in at the house of Mr. Barry, the partner of Mr. Morrison, because once Mr. Morrison very kindly took me on a drive and pointed out the place to me."

Morrison made a vague, snarling sound.

"It was a dark evening," said Rose Taylor. "The clouds were piling up. But Mr. Pollok said that since we had started watching Mr. Morrison, we might as well keep on. There is a little lane just beyond this house, leading up into the woods. We drove the car up there on the edge of the hill. The trees covered the car very well. We walked down through the trees and sat on a log at a place where we could just see the front door of the house without being seen ourselves. The day was ending. We waited quite a time before Mr. Morrison came out and got in his car."

"How did Mr. Morrison seem when he left?" asked Campbell.

"Mr. Morrison looked as though someone had just struck him . . . he seemed a little afraid. He looked smaller than he usually does," said the girl. "His neck seemed to shrink down inside his coat."

She waited. Campbell, glaring at Morrison, defied him silently to make a comment. Morrison was still. He merely pulled out a handkerchief and mopped his face.

"Mr. Morrison drove off," said Rose Taylor, "and we were about to follow when Mr. Pollok said there was no use. Whatever Mr. Morrison had intended to do, he probably had finished doing it now."

Morrison groaned.

The girl looked up at him with her smile. "I really have to tell the whole truth, don't I, Mr. Morrison?" she said.

"Don't pay any attention to him," commanded Campbell. "Go right ahead. Sure you have to tell the whole truth."

"And a moment later, as we were standing up," said Rose Taylor, "a big blue car drove up. It was almost completely dark, now, and a few drops of rain were falling. But by the lantern over the door we were able to see Miss Barry get out of the car and ring the doorbell. I was able to recognize Miss Barry. Her picture had been in the newspapers so often."

She gave Jacqueline one of her smiling, upward glances. But Jacqueline did not smile in return.

"That was when you were seeing the moving picture, wasn't it?" asked O'Rourke. "That was when you were seeing *The First Smile,* Miss Barry?"

She looked at O'Rourke and said nothing. Willett, examining her closely, saw no alteration in her expression. Perhaps her breathing quickened a little.

"Miss Barry went into the house," said Rose Taylor, "and remained there only a short time. I thought that we ought to go back to New York, but Mr. Pollok said he wanted to see what was happening. He went down to the house and looked through a window. He said that a very heated argument was going on between Miss Barry and Mr. Barry. When he returned, Mr. Pollok said that something was in the air and that we should wait and watch.

"He went back to the window. I stayed where I was. It was raining quite hard, by this time. It was hard to see anything except where the light shone out of the windows into the rain. And, of course, there was the lantern over the front door. Miss Barry drove away, and almost at once after her came another car, driving very fast. It stopped at the door and a gentleman got out whom I'd never seen. Mr. Pollok came over and asked if I knew him. Neither had Mr. Pollok seen him before. It was Mr. Willett. He went inside.

"It was raining very hard. I thought surely that we ought to go back to New York, but Mr. Pollok said something was in the air. He brought the robe from the car and we sat under that, but I grew very damp. Mr. Pollok went back down to the house and came back to say that Mr. Willett and Mr. Barry were talking quietly, but that it looked as though Mr. Willett did not like Mr. Barry a very great deal. And then Mr. Willett went away. We waited a few minutes. It seemed a long time. But Mr. Pollok said that he thought that something was still in the air."

"What words did he use?" asked O'Rourke.

"He said that hell was going to pop," said Rose Taylor, and blushed. "He said that he had a sense when trouble was in the air. He said that Mr. Barry was nervous as a mouse when it sees a cat. He said that Mr. Barry was expecting something.

"Another car came. Miss Barry got out of it and went into the house again. She stayed only a short time, and Mr. Pollok watched again at the window. He said that Miss Barry was asking for something and that Mr. Barry was flying into a great rage and shaking his fist. Mr. Pollok came back and told me this, and immediately afterwards Miss Barry left the house. She slammed the door of her car very loudly, I remember."

Everyone looked suddenly at Jacqueline Barry. But she kept her head high. And again her color showed not the slightest alteration. There was a sort of calm menace, perhaps, in her green eyes as she watched the narrator.

Rose Taylor went on, "Other people came. First there was Mr. Telford. Mr. Pollok got up to return to his window and watch, but Mr. Telford came out again almost at once and walked away. Afterwards, Mr. Willett returned."

"Barry had everybody goin' and comin', that night," said O'Rourke. "Sounds like a play. Everybody entering and re-entering. Makes me feel like I was back in school reading Shakespeare, or somebody. Go on, Miss Taylor. You're telling a lot of interesting things."

Rose Taylor lifted her eyes once toward Willett, but her smile was not with the lifting of her eyes.

"Shortly after Mr. Willett arrived," she said, "Mr. Pollok went back to the window. He came running back to me. He said that Mr. David Barry was hanging by the neck from the railing of the balcony . . . and that Mr. Willett was sitting by the fire smoking a cigarette and watching the dead man!"

Her voice had lifted just a little. Her eyes were half closed. O'Rourke stood still. But Campbell drew an automatic from his pocket and stared at Willett.

"Look at her!" said Jacqueline Barry. "See the perfect look of the perfect liar! I was in that house when Mr. Willett entered it!"

Willett lighted a cigarette, carefully, turning it so that the flame would take hold. He lighted the cigarette as though it were a cigar.

Then he said, "Put up the gun, Campbell. I'm not going to run away. I'm not such a fool."

Rose Taylor had needed a bit of time to digest the last comment from Jacqueline Barry. Now she sprang up and cried to O'Rourke, "Sergeant O'Rourke, am I to be insulted . . . just because a woman has money, is she allowed to insult me?"

"You contemptible little blackmailer," said Jacqueline Barry, "did you plan these lies by yourself, or did Pollok help you? They're lies, and they're stupid."

"Oh, are they?" shrilled Rose Taylor. Her voice screeched on a high note. She doubled up her fists. "What are you. . . ."

"Just be quiet, Rose," said O'Rourke. He stared at one girl

and then the other. "Sit down, Rose. We'll get through this all, in time."

He turned to Jacqueline Barry.

"Blackmail?" he said. "Was that the word you used?"

"She came to my house to blackmail me," said Jacqueline.

"That's a lie!" cried Rose.

"Jacqueline, you were not at the Barry house that night, were you?" demanded Telford. He had jumped from his chair. He stood with his hands pressed together, his body inclined slightly forward.

Jacqueline looked at him with unaltered calm.

"Yes, I was there," she said. "I've just stated that I was there."

Telford caught hold of the back of his chair and lowered himself slowly into it. His head had fallen.

26

❖

"Willett Spills the Beans"

"We'll try a time schedule," said Campbell. "According to what you say, Miss Taylor. . . ."

"I've told the absolute truth, word by word," said Rose Taylor. "And because another woman has used her face to advertise a soap I don't see why. . . ."

O'Rourke said: "Steady, Rose. We're not playing any favorites here. We simply want to find out who goes to the electric chair. Go ahead with the time schedule, Angus. We'll get down to the blackmail later on."

Campbell asked, "When do you think that Mr. Morrison arrived at the Barry house, here?"

"About eight o'clock," said Rose, still on fire as she stared at Jacqueline. But the cool, green eyes of Jacqueline were totally oblivious of her existence.

"Eight o'clock," said Campbell, writing. "And he left when?"

"Well, about eight-forty, I suppose."

"And then who came next?" asked Campbell.

"Miss Jacqueline Barry."

"About when?"

"Say a quarter of nine."

"And she stayed how long?"

"Well, about two minutes. A little after nine Mr. Willett arrived. I should say it was a little after nine. He might have been there for fifteen minutes or so. Afterwards came Miss Barry again, perhaps about nine-thirty. She was gone in five minutes, and Mr. Telford came at let's say a quarter of ten. He was gone ten minutes later, and just about ten, Mr. Willett arrived."

Rose was looking at Willett now.

"The medical examiner said that the murder must have taken place about tennish," commented Campbell quietly. "And now let's go back on the trail a little. Mr. Telford, Miss Barry, Mr. Morrison all admit that they were here this evening. Mr. Willett, you admit that you were here?"

"Certainly," said Willett.

"We'll have Miss Barry's story, first. The exact truth, Miss Barry, please."

"How much difference does this all make to you, John?" she asked.

He shook his head and made a gesture. "It's all right," he said, in a husky voice.

"Well, I was here, as I said," she replied. "I can repeat the story twenty times and not take many words. I came because I was head over heels in debt. A year ago I had stocks and cash in my own name, and the bottom fell out of everything. I owed for clothes, automobiles, everything. I was to get a big settlement when I married. I didn't see why my engagement to Mr. Telford should be prolonged, so I came down to talk to Uncle David."

"Take your time," urged O'Rourke, "we like to have people take plenty of time and words, in a case like this. The little things you leave out might be the ones that we want to know. For instance, just what did you say to your uncle?"

"I told him frankly where I stood. He flew into a temper. He said that I was a spendthrift and a worthless girl. He said that I only had brains to spend money and not sense enough to save it or to make it. He fell into such a rage that he said that he had no use for the man I was going to marry."

"Check," said Willett.

Telford turned slowly, regarded Willett, and turned back toward Jacqueline. His face was pale and his lips were stiff. He swallowed but could not put his anger down. The glare of it turned his eyes pale.

The girl, during this interruption, remained expressionless. Her glance drifted toward Telford and then toward Willett, but with the most indifferent consideration.

"Then you left?" asked Campbell.

"Then I left. I stopped at Mr. Telford's house and let him know how the talk had turned out."

"Did he take it hard?" asked O'Rourke.

"No, not in the least. You weren't particularly in favor of a hurried marriage, John, were you?"

"Answer for yourself, not for him," snapped Campbell. "Let's get on."

"I started to drive home, but thinking about what Uncle David had said made me so furious that I decided to go back again and have a last word or two with him. I went back to tell him that I was through with him and his wretched money."

"You went back pretty angry?" said O'Rourke.

"Angrier than I'd ever been in my life."

"Don't say that, Jacqueline!" broke in Telford.

"I'm going to tell the truth," she replied. "I got back to the house and there was no answer when I rang the bell. I pushed at the knob and found that the door hadn't been sent home by the last person through; the bolt hadn't engaged. I went in and I called out for Uncle David to let him know who it was. There wasn't any answer. I walked on into the living room. He wasn't there. Something stirred on the floor. It was only a thin shadow. I looked up and saw him hanging from the balcony . . . *that* balcony."

She did not pause in her quiet narrative.

"Did you scream? Did you yell out?" asked Campbell.

"Scream?" she repeated. "No, I went over to him and looked in his face. By the glaze across his eyes I knew that he was dead. Before I could do anything else, Mr. Willett came in."

"It's not true!" cried Rose Taylor. "She had left . . . she'd driven off in her car before Mr. Willett came!"

"Please, don't interrupt," said Campbell. "Let me get this

157

straight. After you left Mr. Telford's house, you came straight back to this place?"

"No," said Jacqueline Barry. "I started for home, as I said, and I'd driven a distance before my anger got the better of me, and I returned here."

"How far had you gone?" asked Campbell.

"I don't know. I was so angry that I wasn't noticing time and distance very clearly."

"You don't remember anything very well?"

"I remember passing a couple of cars. That's about all."

"You don't remember where you turned?"

"On one of the big north and south highways. It may have been the White Plains Road."

"Then you came back here?"

"Yes."

"Miss Taylor," said Campbell, "you say that after Miss Barry came here and left for the second time, Mr. Telford arrived and then left?"

"I say it . . . I know it . . . I swear that that's exactly what happened!" said Rose Taylor.

"Have you a light, Dick?" asked Jacqueline, picking up a cigarette from an open box of them on the table.

He got up and used his lighter for her. She thanked him with a smile.

Campbell was saying: "Little discrepancy in there. Always find discrepancies when there are dead men around. Miss Barry, you were at the house, you were saying, when Mr. Willett came in?"

"Yes."

"And your uncle was already hanging dead from the balcony?"

"Yes."

"Interesting," said Campbell.

"Yeah, damned if it ain't," murmured O'Rourke.

"What did Mr. Willett do? Cut the body down from the rope?"

"He said simply that Uncle David was dead as a herring. And

158

that he happened to know that he was named in the will for a hundred thousand. He intended to get out of the house and never let a soul know that he'd been there. He advised me to do the same thing. After all, I was the heiress. If we telephoned, he pointed out that there would be a good deal of explaining to manage. It might pass as suicide, but anyone who knew Uncle David knew that he didn't have the courage to commit suicide. His bravery was confined to snarling. And so we left."

"Just like that," said Campbell. "You just walked out and left him hanging there?"

"Are you asking me what I did or what I felt about it?" asked the girl.

"Never mind," answered Campbell. "There's not much feeling in the twentieth-century girl. Anyway, let it go. You've finished your story?"

"Yes. We left the house. He drove off in his car and I in mine."

"There isn't one *word* of truth in it!" exclaimed Rose Taylor.

"We'll come back to the blackmail idea," said Campbell. "What about that, Miss Barry?"

"Miss Taylor came to see me," said Jacqueline, "and told me that she and her man had been hiding in the trees and had seen me come to the house of my uncle on the night of the twenty-second. And that afterwards the man had seen David Barry hanging in the living room. She wanted money. Not a solid, lump sum, but an annuity. About ten thousand a year, after I came into my inheritance, would have suited her, she said."

"Ah, Miss Taylor?" said Campbell.

"She could lie about being at the house; she could lie about being there with Mr. Willett; she can lie about everything!" said Rose Taylor. "I went to see Miss Barry to ask her to buy a block of tickets to the entertainment for the benefit of the East Side dock workers. I told her that there would be a picture in it . . . publicity. If she was willing to advertise soap with her face, I thought she might be willing to advertise dock workers, too."

"How about it, Miss Barry?" asked Campbell.

She was looking steadily at the other girl. She said nothing.

"Quit it, Angus," said O'Rourke. "No use having a cat fight. Mr. Telford, yonder, didn't tell us about seein' Miss Barry, when he talked before."

"Do you think," said Telford, "that I would incriminate Miss Barry?"

"No, that's dumb of me," said O'Rourke.

"According to you, Miss Taylor," said Campbell, "Mr. Willett was the last person into the house, the last person to leave the house, and he was in there alone . . . with David Barry?"

"Yes," said the girl.

"And while you were there, Pollok went to look and came back to tell you that David Barry was hanging by his neck from the balcony, and that Willett was sitting by the fire and smoking a cigarette?"

"That's exactly it," said Rose Taylor.

Willett laughed.

"What a regular sweetheart you are, Rose!" said he.

"Checking it the other way," said Campbell, "Miss Barry says that while she was there . . . with the dead man . . . Mr. Willett came in and found her there. You stalemate each other, the pair of you. And that's where justice is out of luck."

"I've proved that Miss Barry could lie!" said Rose Taylor. "I've proved. . . ."

Willett said: "Rose, you may want to see me in the electric chair, but aren't you rather a fool to balance your word against the word of Miss Barry? Don't do it anymore. It's silly."

"When I want your help . . . ," shouted Campbell, in a rage.

"Be still," said Willett. "You'd make a good rat and get into a lot of obscure holes in the ground if your ears weren't so large. Don't try to silence me when I choose to talk. But I'm ready to give my own story, now, if you're ready to listen to it."

"You talk to him. I'd choke," said Campbell.

O'Rourke said: "Go ahead, Mr. Willett."

160

"I had a letter from Barry. You both saw it. I came out that night in answer to the letter. When I saw Barry, he was in a dead funk. Half crazy with meanness and fear. He asked me to kill him. He said he knew that I hated him enough to kill, which was true. He offered me a Kelmsford automatic to do the job, pointed out that I had not been near him for five years and that no one was apt to suspect me. I asked him why he was in such a panic, and he said that he had heard from John Telford . . . it's coming now, Telford. How do you feel in your rotten, yellow heart?"

Telford had a cigarette going and blew some of the smoke toward Willett, waving his hand after it.

"Go on, Dick," he said. "Tie me into it if you can. I knew you would. But tell me how? That's where I'm curious. It's the kind of lie that I'm interested in, not the dimensions of it."

Willett smiled. The white of his teeth shone through the parted lips.

"Barry told me," he said, "that John Telford had informed him that on the next day the district attorney of New York City was going to open an investigation into the books of the Barry–Morrison firm, and find out about certain sums of money paid out *before* bids on public contracts had been opened . . . contracts that Morrison–Barry secured. How about that, Morrison?"

"Absolute and damnable . . . ," began Morrison.

Willett raised his hand, and Morrison stopped talking, horrified and fascinated.

"Bribery," said Willett, "was of course the order of the day with this pudgy crook of a Morrison. He passed the money . . . but the money was Barry's. No courts in the land would have believed that Barry had not agreed to the dirty work. The thing would spill through the daily papers. 'Philanthropist jailed for bribery.' Sweet, eh? I laughed when I heard it. Barry was sick. I told him to buck up. And I left the house promising to come back.

"I got to a phone in the next town and rang up the district attorney. He told me it was all rot. There was to be no investigation of the Morrison–Barry books and the conduct of their business. He asked me if there ought to be. I laughed and rang off. When I got back to the house, I found Barry dead."

"How about this, Telford?" asked O'Rourke, stepping forward a pace.

Telford shook his handsome head. "You've heard him. Why should I comment?" he asked.

"Get hold of the district attorney," said Willett. "Ask him if I telephoned to his house the night of the twenty-second; when, and about what."

"You're telling the truth, there," said Campbell suddenly. "But what you telephoned may simply have been a plan. It doesn't prove that Telford had said any such thing to Barry. Why should he?"

"Use your brain," said Willett. "He tried to scare Barry to death. And he almost succeeded. When he didn't manage to drive Barry to suicide, he came up and turned the trick with his own hands."

"Ah . . . good! Now I see the line of reasoning," said Telford, nodding his head. "You're a clever fellow, Dick. By the Lord, you really are! Why you're not a billionaire, I can't tell."

"You tell us what happened?" said O'Rourke pleasantly.

"Certainly," said Willett. "It's entirely simple. Telford came to the house, entered, and found Barry alone. Murdered him, and then hanged him from the balcony. He had to manage the thing that same evening. There was no other way out. First he'd seen to it that Jacqueline Barry went to the old devil and tried to persuade him to consent to an early marriage. But Barry wouldn't do that. Why? I'm not quite sure, but I can guess."

"Love to have your guess," said O'Rourke.

"It was probably like this: Barry began to suspect that his firm of Morrison–Barry was not doing as well as it ought to do. He began to make an inquiry . . . not through his lawyer, Telford, but on his own account. He found enough to make him swear that Morrison was a crook and that Telford had covered Morrison's crookedness. How about it, John?"

"Perfectly correct, of course," sneered Telford. "You're wonderful, Dick. Like nature, you're wonderful."

"You see the picture?" said Willett. "Both Morrison and Telford are put into the frying pan. The day after the twenty-second, Barry will finish his investigation of some queer things about his firm. That investigation will show him that Telford is a crook, covering up Morrison and splitting the profits."

Morrison laughed loudly.

"Don't do that again," said Willett. "Not while I'm talking."

"Look!" cried Morrison. "Murder! Did you see his face just then? Murder if I ever saw it!"

"In order to prevent Barry from carrying on, you see all that happens?" said Willett. "Morrison comes out here that evening. He fails. Telford has struck the big blow, the fake about the district attorney's investigation, hoping to drive Barry to suicide. Telford calls in Jacqueline Barry, because if Barry will consent to the marriage at once, it means that he won't dig up any of the dead bones of the past of Telford. Don't you see? I give you the reasons why Morrison, Telford, Miss Barry, and I all arrived at the house on the same evening. Can any of the rest of you give a ghost of a reason why we all arrived at the same time? I tell you, it was because of something that Barry had done . . . he was pulling the house down on his own head."

Telford laughed.

"Like Swanson, eh?" said Campbell.

"It's the sweep of the idea that I like," said Telford. "Notice the sweep and the fervor, Jacqueline?"

He laughed again. But Jacqueline did not laugh. She was too busy watching Willett with her quiet, clear green eyes.

"That's all," said O'Rourke. "You're all free to leave."

"Telford, too?" asked Willett.

27

❖

"Roadside Meeting"

Campbell said: "We should have arrested somebody."
"Why didn't you do it, then?" asked O'Rourke.
"Now that they're gone, go run after them and bring 'em to jail. I don't give a damn what you do."

Campbell paid no attention to the outburst. He repeated: "We should have arrested somebody. Hell is going to pop, now that they're all turned loose together."

"What kind of hell?" asked O'Rourke.

Campbell grew weary. He said: "Your little sweetheart, Rose Taylor, is ready to stick a knife into Jacqueline Barry. And no snake had greener eyes than Jacqueline Barry when she looked at Rose. Telford and Willett hate each other up to the murder point. And Morrison's the kind of coward that kills in a panic."

"Arrest five people on suspicion?" asked O'Rourke.

Campbell was silent, slowly shaking his head.

"There's no way out, just now," said O'Rourke. "We gotta wait for these eggs to unscramble themselves for a while."

"Who was lying the most?" wondered Campbell. "Rose or Jacqueline? If Rose tells the truth, Willett's the only one who could have turned the trick, I suppose. If Jacqueline tells the truth it couldn't be Willett; it must be herself or Morrison, or Telford."

"There's a three-to-one bet," said O'Rourke.

"There's another way of looking at it," said Campbell. "All five of them had reasons for wishing Barry out of the way."

"All five except Rose," said O'Rourke.

"She lived on Morrison's money. Morrison is being put on the spot by Barry. With Barry out of the way, Morrison keeps on handing out the hard cash. Yes, all five of them had reasons for wishing to see Barry dead. What if they all threw their hands in together to kill Barry?"

"They're not helping now," said O'Rourke. "They're trying to dig knives into each other."

"Maybe that's a bluff. They pretend to hate each other so's to keep us from thinking that they're in cahoots. But suppose that they worked this all out together and then arranged to give testimony that would make all one big confusion. Notice how it goes? What one man says cancels out the rest. They're the only witnesses, and they help one another by being different."

"That's an idea," declared O'Rourke. "Where do we go from here, Angus?"

"Think for yourself!" said Campbell. "My brain's empty from trying to get a new hunch."

JACQUELINE BARRY was a fast driver, but as she entered the little crossroads that led toward her house, with the headlights shimmering down the double line of trees that bordered the driveway, another car went by her with a moan of speed. Brakes groaned. The road was blocked in a narrow place and she had to stop in her turn.

She unbuttoned the side pocket of the roadster and pulled a gun out of it. She could see the awkward figure of a man climbing out into the spray of her headlight. It was Willett who came back toward her. She held the automatic with a firmer grip, for a moment. Then she laid it down on the seat beside her. Willett came up and opened the driver's door. He put one knee on the running board, which leveled him with her sitting height.

"That was a useful lie you told tonight," he said. "Why did you do it?"

"You gave me back a handkerchief and you got the yellow dress for me," she answered.

"Telford is going down and I'm coming up," said Willett. "Isn't that the truth? Do you think that I could have killed Barry?"

"Yes," she said. "Do you think that I could?"

"Yes," said Willett. "The other thing is, what about you and me?"

"In what sense?"

"Jacqueline," he said, "you're more than five minutes old. This is a love scene, young fellow."

"One of the new kind, Richard?"

"When I heard you lying for me," said he, "it did something to me."

"Go on," said Jacqueline.

"Do you like it?"

"Yes."

"You did something more to me than coffee on a cold morning or bacon and eggs after a hungry day. . . . That's a love speech, if you look at it in the right way."

"Yes, it is," said Jacqueline.

He put out an arm. She leaned forward and fitted it around her.

"The instrument board doesn't give much light," said Willett, "but I can see you by the hammering of your heart. This means something to you, I think."

"It does," said Jacqueline.

"You're not making just a friendly gesture, are you?" he asked.

"That's all it is, Richard."

"I don't believe it. You're not the type. You don't let the lads amuse themselves of an evening by mauling you around."

"No," she admitted.

"But you want me here, isn't that right?"

"Yes," she said.

"And when you told the lie for me tonight, something like a door opened up in your heart and let in a lot of new ideas?"

"Yes."

"The Telford scheme got far away and dim, didn't it?"

"Yes," she admitted.

"Then to hell with Telford," said Willett, "and here's where we start."

He lowered his face until he could feel her breathing. Then he waited.

"Is this our beginning?" he asked.

"It's our ending, Richard," she said.

"Don't try to use the brain. Damn the brain!" said Willett. "What does the old instinct say?"

"It speaks for you till my heart aches!"

"I can take the ache away."

"I know you can."

"I'm not going to kiss an early Christian martyr, though. Can't you be a little more than patient?"

"I can be, but I won't."

"What's the matter, Jacqueline?"

"If you and I tried life together, don't you know what would happen?"

"The kind of happiness we'd show the world would make other people pretty sick. When they saw us, they'd want to start all over again. Men would change their minds about things and go hunting for the real women. Married people would get married over again for luck."

"Ah!" said Jacqueline.

"Isn't it true?" asked Willett.

She said: "We'd have children with quicksilver in their bodies and in their eyes."

"They'd knock holes in things," said Willett. "We'll get married tomorrow."

"No, we won't. We're saying good-bye!"

"Don't lie to me, Jacqueline."

"I'm not lying."

"Why are you here inside my arms, talking about saying good-bye? Wait a moment. You think it's the damned money I'm after?"

"Partly, perhaps," she said.

"It's not, though," said Willett.

"If you say so, then the money doesn't count. I want to believe that."

"Jacqueline, you're trembling. Isn't that love?"

"Yes, it is."

"Then what's all this nonsense about saying good-bye?"

"We're a pair of bad ones. If we married, we'd go smash, crash to hell."

"I'd hold you up by the hair of the head. I wouldn't let you go."

"You couldn't. You'd have to follow me. I'd have to follow you. We'd go crash. . . . Listen, Richard. I've always known that there was the devil in me. Nobody could keep me walking a straight line except a cold-minded man like John Telford."

"You're talking like a fool, Jacqueline."

"Could you trust me?"

"Of course I could."

"Trust me absolutely, I mean? Could you tell that the right thoughts were pattering along inside my mind like little children coming straight home from school?"

"I wouldn't give a damn for such a woman."

"Isn't there a suspicion in your brain that I may have killed David Barry?"

"No," said Willett.

"Tell me honestly. The way I'll try to tell you. Isn't there a suspicion?"

"Yes," said Willett. "And you suspect the same of me?"

"It hardly matters whether one or the other of us did the thing. The point is that we *could* have done it, either of us."

"Wait a minute. I'm strong enough to keep us both straight."

"You couldn't," she said. "Then there's another thing. But I can't talk about it."

"You can talk about anything."

"It's like this. Now that I'm here in your arms . . . yes, and even before . . . even tonight, when I looked at you and knew all at once that I loved you . . . I could feel a child of your blood in my body . . . even the weight and the stirring of it here

168

under my heart. But if ever we had children, I'd be in mortal fear every day of my life. I'd be afraid of seeing the Richard devil or the Jacqueline devil look out of their eyes. My fear would make them hate me . . . would make *you* hate me. And if you hate anyone, you can be a cruel devil, Richard."

"Yes, I can," said he.

"You see that it wouldn't be a go?"

"I'd make a go of it if I had to crack open hell and let the daylight into it."

"Richard, we're saying good-bye. Will you kiss me?"

"That would be a little too thick," said Willett.

He stood back.

"Richard!" she cried out.

He went on silently to his car and got into it. The engine started with a roar. He turned the machine and shot it back. Its fender clanged like a bell against the nearer mudguard of the girl's automobile. He was gone, stepping the gears smoothly up into top speed.

28

❖

"O'Rourke Makes
an Arrest"

O'Rourke said: "It's pretty late and I'm fagged, Rose. Be a good girl and give me a drink, and then I'd like to hear everything you want to say about Mr. Willett."

"And the other man," said the girl. "The man who's with Mr. Willett at his house now."

"Slogger Haines? Oh, you got something on him?"

She went out and brought in a tray of drinks before she answered the last question.

"I hope I haven't anything on anyone, Mr. O'Rourke," she said. "But I just sort of feel that I ought to tell all the truth exactly as I know it."

"That's because you're a real good girl, Rose," said O'Rourke, and he washed down his words with a slug of Scotch. Then he was able to add, "Go right ahead, Rose."

"It was about Mr. Willett being here the day that Mr. Pollok was killed," said Rose, sighing. She looked out the window toward the wavering lights on the East River. A train rolled soft thunder over the bridge. "Everything in life seems so hard and so confused for a girl, Mr. O'Rourke."

"Yeah. I bet it does," said O'Rourke. "You gotta watch where you step, is what you gotta do."

"Isn't that true?" breathed Rose.

"Let's start with what Willett was doing here that day," said O'Rourke.

"It was all quite a tangle. . . . You see, Mr. O'Rourke, I'm

170

afraid that Mr. Pollok wasn't a really good man. He wanted to use what he had learned at the Barry house, the night of the twenty-second. He wanted to get money from the people who were there, it seems. And he must have got in touch with Mr. Willett. I suppose Mr. Willett put agents to watch Mr. Pollok and discovered that I knew him. Anyway, Mr. Willett came here."

"Well, what did he have in mind?"

"Not very nice things," said Rose. "You see . . . I was alone . . . well, that's done and forgotten. But chiefly I think he wanted to make sure that I would be here and that I wouldn't go to Mr. Pollok's room and perhaps interfere in what was to happen."

"What makes you think that?" asked O'Rourke, pouring another drink.

"I saw Mr. Willett, shortly after he arrived, go to the window and make a signal, and at once a man across the street walked away. That man across the street was Slogger Haines!"

"Was he? Ah!"

"And then, afterwards, Mr. Pollok telephoned me . . . and, while he was telephoning, I heard the shot that killed him!"

"The devil! What was Pollok saying?"

"I don't remember. Nothing important. And then the shot came . . . and I heard the receiver click up while I was screaming: 'Sid! Sid!' Oh!" She covered her face with her hands.

Sergeant O'Rourke bit off the end of a cigar, watching her without any great sympathy.

"Cheer up, Rose," he said. "Pollok was a bum."

"But it was so terrible!" said Rose, looking up sadly.

"The idea," said O'Rourke, "is that Willett came here to hold down this end of the line and see that Pollok didn't get the wrong visit. Once he was here, he waved Haines to go and bump off Pollok?"

"It seems that way, doesn't it?" asked Rose.

"Yeah; maybe, maybe," said O'Rourke. "Willett, when he was up here, got kind of familiar with you, did he?"

Rose shuddered.

"Kind of got to handling you?" asked O'Rourke.

She nodded.

"You didn't make a yell or anything?"

"I pleaded with him," said Rose.

"What a damned little two-faced liar you are!" said O'Rourke. "I know men, sweetheart. Willett's not that kind. So good night to you!"

He left at once, and drove straight to the house of Willett. He had to ring several times before the door was dragged open by Slogger Haines, who was rubbing his eyes.

"Sorry, governor, I must of . . . ," began the Slogger.

He halted when he recognized the detective.

"Slogger Haines," said O'Rourke, "I arrest you for the murder of Sidney Pollok. Come with me!"

He had his hand on a gun in his coat pocket. The Slogger reached out with amazing speed and gripped the wrist of O'Rourke's gun hand. O'Rourke put three useless bullets into the wall while the Slogger hit him behind the ear. O'Rourke's forefinger slipped from the trigger. Only echoes flew up and down the street. The Slogger struck again. O'Rourke slipped to his knees. He did not feel the third blow that crumpled him in a heap on the little porch.

When he awakened, someone was shaking him by the arm. Willett leaned over him, breathing sweet whiskey fumes.

"Have a fall?" said Willett. "Here's the door open and no Slogger to answer the bell. What's the matter?"

He helped O'Rourke to his feet.

"You're a little wobbly on the pins, Sergeant. Come inside with me."

He had to carry half of the weight of the detective until they reached the living room. Then O'Rourke found his feet. He used them to get to a chair into which he sank.

"That Slogger has a good right hand," said O'Rourke, "and he used it on me. Any lumps on my mug?"

"Nothing I can see. Yes, when you turn your face. Why did you stir up the Slogger? He's a good-natured boy, usually."

"Let's talk about something else," said O'Rourke. "The Taylor girl doesn't love you too much, Mr. Willett."

"Has she been barking up my tree again?" asked Willett.

"She don't care a whole lot for you," said O'Rourke.

"She's as pretty a girl as I ever saw," said Willett. "She has that childish purity, the little touch of heaven in the eyes and the mouth."

"D'you like her?"

"Like her? It isn't a question of liking, is it?" chuckled Willett.

"Will you talk to me, Big Boy?"

"I'm trotting right along with you," pointed out Willett.

"Maybe Rose liked you a little too much for a while. She hates your gizzard, now."

"She showed that when we were out at the Barry house."

"How much truth did she talk?"

"You make up your mind about that," said Willett.

"Will you tell me if she ever talked pretty kind to you, like she needed a home and a man about the house?" asked O'Rourke.

"I don't know anything about that," said Willett.

"I think you do," said O'Rourke. "When a gal like Rose gets poisonous, it's because somebody has slapped her face in a brand-new way. You sent her about her business."

"Business is the right word. Rose is a capable girl."

"Willett, I could do you some good, maybe, if you'd talk."

"You mean that you want me to talk about Rose?"

"Why not?"

"I never talk about women, O'Rourke."

"Wait a minute. When I say that this is important, I mean what I say."

"You're a good fellow," answered Willett, "but I'm not going to talk about the Taylor girl, or any other."

"I see that's final. Will you tell me where I can look up Slogger Haines?"

"I don't know. He used to live uptown, somewhere. Somewhere rather near to the North River. That's all I can tell you about where he might be. You think he's left that front door open for good?"

"I think he has," said O'Rourke.

"You're wrong," said Willett. "He'll come back. He won't leave me."

"Wait and see," said the detective. "Sorry you won't talk. Damned sorry. So long, Mr. Willett."

"Hot and cold water will take down those bumps," said Willett.

"I leave 'em for the inspector," declared O'Rourke. "When a man gets fat, he's got to keep proving every little while that he's still one of the boys. So long, Mr. Willett. Good luck to you. A lot of good luck."

He went out into the street and climbed into his car. Every time a traffic light stopped him on the way down town he shook his head and said: "Funny damn thing! Funny damn thing!"

29

❖

"The Confession"

The newspapers carried the Slogger Haines alarm on the front page, as a rule. The notice was short. It was definite that Haines was wanted for the murder of Pollok.

On an inside page there was a description of the burial of the celebrated philanthropist David Barry. Most of the article went to the events of the life of Barry and to the list of his benefactions. It appeared that St. Edmund's School for Boys had been in expectation of a huge two-million-dollar endowment fund; St. Edmund's School was deeply shocked to learn of the death of their would-be benefactor. St. Edmund's School was confident that the noble-heartedness of the heirs of Mr. Barry would compel them to execute what was really his dying wish and manifest intention. The intention could be proved by a glance through recent correspondence with Mr. Barry.

As for the burial itself, it had small space. Not many people had come. Miss Barry was there. John Telford was there. The newspaper did not even mention Matilda Grunsky, in her best clothes and her brightest smile.

The town of Farmhaven intended to put up a monument to David Barry. A public subscription had been opened for the purpose of securing sufficient funds.

"Does it make good reading?" asked Campbell, coming to O'Rourke's desk.

O'Rourke stacked his feet on top of the blotter at the edge of his desk.

"St. Edmund's School will have a hot chance of getting two millions out of Jacqueline Barry," said O'Rourke. "You wouldn't see a little extra motive in this, somewheres? The heirs wanting to chip off the old man before he had the chance to throw away some more of his money for the sake of head-lines?"

"Maybe," said Campbell.

"Sure, 'maybe,' " said O'Rourke. "Telford and Jacqueline Barry would have plenty of reason, if they heard about it, and they sure would have heard. But here's something on the Barry case."

He pushed a letter across the desk.

Campbell picked it up and read:

To Sergeant Patrick O'Rourke:
   Please note that the David Barry case is apparently plain sui-cide. File the case and inform Sergeant Campbell. . . .

"The damn fool!" said Campbell.

"All inspectors are that way," said O'Rourke. "If they had any brains, they wouldn't be inspectors."

"We've got the Slogger Haines angle to work on, though," said Campbell. "If what little Rose told you the other day is right, we're going to put Haines on the spot. And that case runs right back into the Barry muddle. What bit the inspector to make him write that note, though?"

"The dirty books of the Morrison–Barry firm. The district attorney is opening up on Morrison. Going to make an exam-ple of him, he says. And if Morrison–Barry actually offered bribes . . . as they sure did . . . then Barry had a first-rate reason for committing suicide. Did you hear Willett's lingo about that the other night?"

"Willett's a smart man," said Campbell. "When he burns in the chair, a lot of brains are going to fry. What you been doing all day?"

"Working up Slogger Haines. I've got a number of the boys searching, but it looks as though they've got to go over the whole of Harlem and the Bronx to get a lead on him. For a big man, he sure can crowd himself into a small space."

176

"Take the whole job all the way through, and how do you feel about it, Pat?"

"I feel as though I'm working in too much Scotch mist."

"And they've put me in an Irish bog," said Campbell bitterly.

He rubbed the baldness of his head and looked at O'Rourke with unutterable disgust.

The telephone rang. O'Rourke picked it up.

"Speaking to Sergeant O'Rourke?" said a voice.

"Clear your throat," said O'Rourke. "Yes, this is Sergeant O'Rourke. Whatcha want?"

"I'm Slogger Haines," said the dim voice.

O'Rourke looked with a sudden brightness toward Campbell and then, squinting, toward the darkness of the windows and the dazzle of the highlights in them.

"I hear you, Slogger," said O'Rourke, "but only just. Can't you make it clearer? Where are you?"

"I'm half a step from being dead," said the voice in the telephone. "I seen the papers and I guess you'll get me. I killed Pollok, but you birds ain't never gonna get me. You hear? I'm dead damn quick after I finish this talk. I killed Pollok. But it was Willett that put me up to it."

O'Rourke, sitting on the edge of his chair, was writing down with lightning rapidity on his desk blotter the words that were spoken.

"Willett did that, did he?" asked O'Rourke.

"He gave me a thousand dollars and a boost at the Garden, but he didn't do it for nothing. I had to knock over Pollok for him, because Pollok had seen him kill David Barry and was asking for dough. Willett gives me the wallet and the cash in it to plant on Pollok after I done him in. That was to make the police think that Pollok had killed Barry. . . . All right. You've got me, and I'm going to go to hell ahead of the electric chair. But, for God's sake, get that hound Willett! He done the whole thing! So long."

The telephone clicked as the receiver was hung up. O'Rourke kept on writing on the pad. When he finished, he

177

read the entire speech aloud, together with his own interpolations. There were three other detectives in the big room. None of them looked up as the soft voice of O'Rourke read out the message.

As O'Rourke finished the reading, he drew a great scrawling line under the stagger of his writing on the blotter and then leaned back in his chair.

His eyes were closed as he said: "So there it is, Campbell, eh?"

Campbell, having heard the words, came over and stared at them with his own hungry eyes.

"So there it is!" said Campbell. "Willett . . . I knew it was him! I seen it at the first look. I knew . . . I said so, didn't I? But the Irish bog weighted me down a little. My God, the inspector is gonna tie me to you closer than ever, after this. He won't know that I was the one who saw through that tangle all alone. I've got to split up the credit with you. You get half . . . a thick-headed Irishman that was always in a fog. . . ."

O'Rourke opened his eyes.

"It's funny," he said.

"That you should horn in on this? Sure it's funny."

"The Slogger . . . talking," said O'Rourke.

"He's damn near a gorilla, but he could talk English, of a sort," answered Campbell. "I'm going out!"

"Stay here. We'll get reports before long," replied O'Rourke. Then he added, "It was Willett, eh?"

"He always had the face for murder. I was the one that saw that."

"Ahh-h, shut up," advised O'Rourke. "Maybe you had the hunch, this time. Slogger talking, is what beats me."

"What else would he do?"

"Go and try to bash in the skull of Willett. That would be more natcheral, I'd say. Or cut and run with Willett to show him the way. A dummy like Slogger . . . he'd be more likely to lean on Willett in a pinch than to give him away."

"You never can tell," said Campbell. "When a man makes up his mind to kill himself, everything else he does is likely to be queer."

30

❖

"In the Flytrap"

O'Rourke took the telephone and said: "Give me the morgue."

Then he was saying: "Detective Sergeant O'Rourke talking. Body is likely to be picked up, somewhere. In the river, maybe. Big fellow. Two hundred and something. Six feet. Heavy mug. Small eyes. No forehead. That will be Slogger Haines. Let me know."

He hung up the telephone.

"Sitting here and waiting. That's another funny part of it," said O'Rourke.

He took the telephone again and got the office of the medical examiner.

"If you're called to look at a stiff—he gave the description of the Slogger again—"call Detective Sergeant O'Rourke or Campbell. Let us get to the place quick."

As he hung up, Campbell was saying: "It's knowing the mugs as you see them that counts more than anything else. That's how I spotted Willett at the first."

"Aw, hell," said O'Rourke, "don't be too wise after luck plays into your hands. I've seen as many mugs as you. What about Jacqueline, that stood to get the money? What about Telford, that stood to share it with her? The girl is pretty hard and steady, Angus."

"Ay, but the breeding was against her doing anything like that. You train 'em up right and though they may have hell in them, it don't come out so easy. She was trained. That's all. But Telford . . . there's something kind of high and noble about him, O'Rourke, and it was Telford *you* picked."

The telephone rang. A voice over it said: "Sergeant O'Rourke?"

"Yeah."

"Bennett speaking."

"What you find? Nothing, Bennett?"

"Found a room, but nobody in it."

"Haines's room?"

"Yeah, but he ain't there."

"Been there lately?"

"Yeah, he's been there lately. There's still a staleness of pipe tobacco in the air. Magazine open on his table where he was reading a story about the South Seas and. . . ."

"Aw, shut up and say something. What is it, lodging house?"

"Yeah, lodging house. Meals, too."

"Can't you say 'boarding house' right off, and be done with it?"

"All right, Sergeant."

"What they say about him in the house?"

"Kind of a funny mug that never talked much at meals."

"Didn't they see the papers?"

"Yeah, and when the Slogger come home they was gonna tell the cop on the beat.

"Why didn't they telephone headquarters to say that he lived with them?"

"These kind of guys, they got no brains. They don't think," said the detective.

"Stir around and see where he's gone," said O'Rourke.

He hung up.

"Empty coop?" said the Scotchman.

"Yeah, empty."

"We got time," said Campbell. "Who pinches Willett?"

"You do . . . and be damned to you," said O'Rourke. "Do it all by yourself and be happy."

When Willett got back to his place just at ten-thirty and unlocked the door he turned on the hall lights and saw that he had illumined three men who sat in chairs in the narrow of the hallway.

One of them was Detective Sergeant Campbell, who stood up and said: "Arresting you in the name of the law, Mr. Willett. You'll come quietly, won't you?"

"Certainly," said Willett. "What's the charge?"

"Murder and subornation to murder," said Campbell. "I guess it's the chair and a short burn, Mr. Willett."

Willett smiled. He didn't have the look of a man who was afraid of death.

"Maybe," said Willett. "I'll write a note for my friend before I leave."

"You'll come with us," said Campbell.

"I'll write a note to my friend," said Willett.

"Well . . . all right," answered Campbell. He had a gun in his hand and was not trying to conceal it. He walked right behind Willett. One of the other detectives walked in the lead. The third brought up the rear. They went into the library.

"You'll find drinks over on the sideboard, boys," said Willett. And he sat down at a table and pulled paper out of a drawer.

The two detectives looked at the sideboard and then at the sergeant.

"Hell, no," said Campbell. "What you think?"

Willett wrote, with Campbell's eye on the writing:

Dear Bill:
They're picking me up for murder.

He looked up. "Murder of what?" he asked.

"Murder of David Barry," said the sergeant.

They want me for the murder of David Barry. I didn't have that pleasure, but the police have to think their way for a time. Enjoyed your place a lot, and hope you find everything in good shape. Come down and see me in jail unless I get bailed out before you return. Kindest regards.

Dick

He put a book over the edge of the paper and stood up. He dusted his big, hard hands together.

"All right, boys," he said. "Ready to start the little procession?"

"You've got a lot of trust in lawyers," said Campbell. "But you're going to be all washed up before we're through with you. We've got you, Willett."

"You like your job, don't you?" said Willett.

"I like it fine when it means catching murderers," said Campbell. "If you don't mind, I'll put this pair of bracelets on you, Mr. Willett. I've got a lot more respect for your hands than you think I may have."

They went out the front door.

"Is this all?" murmured one of the younger detectives to the other. "Is this the hard-boiled mug we heard about?"

"Yeah, but what's he gonna do?" asked the second. "This ain't the Wild West. Automatics make a hell of a big difference when they got the drop on you. Besides, maybe he's got a stack of law up his sleeve."

THE TELEPHONE CALL had said: "We're holding the crowd back. Slogger Haines is here, dead . . . fell off the bluff. Come right up Riverside Drive."

O'Rourke got there as fast as his machine would rip the distance. He could mark the spot from a distance. It was where the Drive looped back to the side in a byway that ran out toward the main highway. Trees in the parking lot helped to screen the spot. Automobiles were slipping away from the place. Two or three hundred people were milling about. A central core of patrolmen held them back, waving their hands threateningly toward the rash ones. O'Rourke ran his car as close as possible and parked.

Above the spot, the bank sloped over several retreating yards of rugged boulders and above this section the cliff arose in a sheer lift of a hundred feet. A street light burned up there. It helped to illumine the high, rigid back of an apartment house fifteen stories tall. It showed the little bars of a fence, and gleamed green on the side of a tree.

"The Slogger picked a good place," said O'Rourke. "This is the sort of a spot he would have made his header from, all right."

He went up through the crowd. A policeman started to say: "Stand back, Fatty."

"All right, kid," said O'Rourke. "I'm Sergeant O'Rourke."

"Excuse me, Sergeant."

"That's all right, brother. Medical examiner arrived?"

"He's just here."

O'Rourke walked over to the place. He waved to the lieutenant who was on the spot. He nodded to the man kneeling by the body when the doctor looked up.

"I don't see what all the shouting's for," said the medical examiner. "Do I have to leave the table every time a nut takes a high dive at a stretch of pavement? What's the matter with you, O'Rourke?"

"We needed to have a good look at this bird in the spot where he flopped," said O'Rourke. "He tipped us off he was going to do it; only he didn't say when or where. Kind of smeared himself, didn't he?"

"He hit himself with several blunt instruments," said the doctor, standing up.

"Meaning the rocks and then the pavement, eh?"

"Meaning that," said the doctor.

"How long has he been dead?"

"Do I have to go into that? Who is this fellow, anyway?"

"No pal of mine, but he's sending another man to the electric chair with the chatter he handed over the telephone. How long ago, about?"

The doctor wanted to get away.

"Well, wait a minute. I can't tell you to the minute. You know that."

"I know that, of course."

"What time is it now, O'Rourke?"

"It's ten-forty."

"This fellow took his dive about . . . well . . . about an hour and a half ago."

"And a half, did you say?"

"Yes, what about it? Why shout?"

"Wait a minute," said O'Rourke "Any you boys got the precisely right time on you?"

"I have," said the doctor. "It's exactly ten forty-three."

"You couldn't move the time up a little?" asked O'Rourke. "You couldn't make it a little less than an hour ago that the mug jumped over the cliff?"

"Why should I make it less than an hour? I told you before . . . wait a moment."

He repeated his examination with an almost tender care. Then the doctor stood up again and shrugged his shoulders.

"About nine-ten or nine-twenty," said the examiner, "Slogger Haines jumped over this cliff and, as I said before, struck himself on some blunt instruments. Anything else?"

"Not a thing in the world!" said O'Rourke.

He had been in great haste as he drove uptown.

He was equally leisurely in returning downtown.

It was half an hour later before he managed to get in touch with Campbell. The Scotchman had an air of quiet satisfaction.

"The funny thing is," said O'Rourke, "that you get a lot of pleasure out of your work, Angus."

"Irishmen never understood what it means to serve the law," answered Campbell. "I've just left your friend, Willett."

"Where did you put him?"

"In the Flytrap."

"Why the Flytrap? You think that a brain like Willett is going to chatter to itself?"

"Why not? The bigger they are the harder. . . ."

"Angus, I've got something to tell you."

"Save it for tomorrow. I need some sleep. By the way, I've got your scrap of blotter that you wrote the telephone message down on."

"It's not worth a damn," said O'Rourke.

"Isn't it? It's enough to burn friend Willett, though," said Campbell.

"The man with the murder-face, eh?" said O'Rourke, smiling. "Well, sit down and let me talk to you a minute."

Campbell did not sit down. He merely leaned on the back of a chair and said, wearily, "All right. Go ahead."

O'Rourke stepped closer. He even leaned a hand intimately on the thin shoulder of the Scotchman.

As he talked, Campbell began to purse his lips. When the narrative had ended, he emitted a long, slow whistle.

"Well?" said O'Rourke.

"Do we keep our faces shut?" demanded Campbell, suddenly.

"Why not?" asked O'Rourke.

"Yeah, and why not," echoed Campbell. "But the Flytrap?"

"Sure," said O'Rourke. "Don't be dumb. Sure, the Flytrap."

He went out of the room. Campbell remained in his former position, leaning on the back of the chair, staring dreamily into space.

31

❖

"Campbell Sets a Trap"

Campbell sat in the parlor. It could not be called a living room; it was too small, too tight, too regularly ordered. It was the year 1885 held over to 1935, that room. The half century had been waved back in order to put the round table in the center of the floor and the well-dusted knickknacks in the cabinet in the corner. Mrs. Partridge, in her high-necked dress, could have been a transfer out of that older time, too.

Campbell said, "It's about that fellow Haines, you see."

"It was horrible," said Mrs. Partridge.

"It'll make business for you. It'll advertise you," said Campbell.

"Do you think so?" asked Mrs. Partridge.

"Any kind of publicity is good publicity . . . if you don't have to pay for it. Look at what the papers say: 'Respectable boarding house . . . interviewed Mrs. Partridge, the lady-like owner of the place . . . she spoke quietly and well.' All of those things make a good send-off, eh?"

"My parents," said Mrs. Partridge, "always took the greatest care of. . . ."

"What I wanted to know," said Campbell, "was about Haines after he came here."

"He was a quiet sort of a man," said Mrs. Partridge. "At the table he looked down into his plate mostly. He had a terrible way of grinding his bread to pieces between his thumb and forefinger. That was all. I suppose one of these psychologists might have seen that that meant violence and brutality. But I'm an old-fashioned woman, Sergeant Campbell, and I never dreamed that. . . ."

"He never had much company, Mrs. Partridge?"

"Hardly a soul."

"See anyone a day or two ago?"

"Only one man a couple of days ago."

"Who was the man?"

"It was the dark of the twilight. You know, when the light's tricky. Just between day and night, when one isn't used to the electric light yet. And the hall is a little dim, too. He just came in and asked for Mr. Haines. A very gentleman-like–looking man, I thought. So I sent him right upstairs. I waited down in the hall. I heard him knock at the door. I heard Mr. Haines speak to him and then. . . ."

"What did Haines say?"

"He used an oath, Sergeant."

"I can stand it if you can," said Campbell.

"He said: 'Well, I'll be damned! Is it you?' "

"And then what?"

"And then the door closed. That was all I heard."

"When did the stranger leave?"

"Oh, about half an hour later, I suppose."

"Did you have a better look at him when he left?"

"No. I didn't see him at all. I just heard."

"If I showed you some pictures of men, would you be able to identify his face?"

"No," said Mrs. Partridge.

"Tall or short?"

"Tall, Sergeant."

"Big in the shoulders?"

"Yes. Very big."

"That's all you can remember?"

"Yes."

"What made you think he was a gentleman?"

"He had a deep, quiet voice."

"That all you can say?"

"Was he terribly important in the case?"

188

"I don't know. He might be everything, and he might be nothing. . . . All the time that Haines was here, what was the strangest thing that you ever noticed about him . . . aside from his crumbling of the bread?"

"There wasn't anything else, aside from just meeting him, one day."

"Meeting him where?"

"Passing him, I ought to say. Just before dinner I saw that I was short of bread and I hurried out to the store. It's two blocks away, you know. And when I turned the first corner I saw Mr. Haines standing in the middle of the block talking to a girl." She paused.

"He was young enough to talk to a girl," said Campbell. "What sort of a looking girl?"

"That was what struck me first. The sun slanted into her hair and it was bright, bright gold. I walked right past them, then, though I'd intended to walk on the other side of the street."

"You had a good look at her?"

"She was one of the most beautiful girls I ever saw. Blue-eyed. And she was flirting, Sergeant. I mean, when she looked up at Mr. Haines, she smiled in a sudden way. I mean, she was well-dressed, and I wouldn't have thought . . . I mean to say. . . ."

"That's all right," said Campbell. "She had a sudden sort of smile when she looked up; she was small?"

"Yes, rather."

"Very bright golden hair?"

"Yes. Very."

"Blue eyes . . . big ones?"

"Yes, very big."

Campbell pulled some pictures out of his pocket.

"Was this the girl?" he asked.

"Why, Sergeant Campbell! How wonderful of you!" said Mrs. Partridge.

"Yeah, we've got to be wonderful," said Campbell.

It was nearly noon when he reached the apartment of Rose Taylor. But she was still in a dressing gown, with her hair pleasantly tousled, her face rosy from a good sleep.

"Why, Sergeant Campbell!" she said, holding the door ajar. "Are you coming in?"

"If I may," said Campbell.

He stood in the center of the big room.

"I'm only here for a minute," he said. "I've got some bad news for you, Rose. I feel friendly toward you, d'you see, so I thought that I'd come and tell you."

"Oh, how kind of you," said Rose Taylor. "What is the bad news, Sergeant Campbell?"

"I'll tell you straight. I don't get on very well with O'Rourke, y'understand?"

"I've noticed that," said Rose. "He's such a *brutal* man, Sergeant Campbell. A man with a refined face like yours couldn't have anything in common with such a person."

"Thanks," said Campbell. "The point is that O'Rourke has some mean ideas about the Willett case. Fool ideas . . . but mean ones. You been following it this morning?"

He picked up the newspaper that lay on the table. The thing began on the front page . . . the story of the telephoned message to the detectives, and the jump of Slogger Haines from the cliff.

"You've read it?" asked Campbell.

"Poor Mr. Willett!" said the girl. "*What* could have been in his mind?"

"There's the main idea," said Campbell. "O'Rourke is so set on making Willett innocent that he's working along other lines. You understand? He's been trailing you, specifically. All these days. Had you watched every moment."

"Me?" said the girl. "Oh, but how strange of Sergeant O'Rourke!"

"All Irishmen are damned strange," said Campbell. "He got pretty interested about some of the things that you done. Like when you went to see Slogger Haines, for instance."

"Ah?" said Rose.

She was rigid for a moment. Then she shrugged her shoulders. "It made me angry . . . just for an instant . . . ," she said.

190

"I mean to think of being trailed all the time."

"Why *did* you go to see the Slogger?" asked Campbell.

"I suppose that *does* seem strange," she said. "But you know I wanted to face him and ask him, point-blank, if he ever had anything against poor Sidney Pollok. I really did follow him several times from the house where Mr. Willett had been staying. I followed Mr. Haines and finally I overtook him, one day."

"Where was it?"

"Oh, away up north in town . . . I don't remember exactly where. Everything seems so alike, up there."

"And you asked him?"

"Yes."

"What did he do?"

"He gave a frightful start. He looked at me with terrible eyes. But I was standing in the open street. His hands worked. And his mouth worked. But that was all he could do. I was frightened, though, and I got away from him as quickly as I could."

"Why didn't you tell the police about this?" asked Campbell.

"When Sergeant O'Rourke was here, I wanted to tell him about it," she said. "But it was *very* hard to talk to Sergeant O'Rourke."

"Yeah, he's got a mean way about him, sometimes," said Campbell. "But things are getting pretty confused. The way it stands now, I wouldn't tell anybody else about meeting Slogger Haines. They might think it was funny . . . the question you wanted to ask him."

"But he confessed, finally, that he was a murderer," she said.

"No, he didn't," answered Campbell.

"But here in the newspaper. . . ."

"The man who telephoned in the name of Slogger Haines wasn't Haines at all."

"Oh!" she cried.

"There was a little mix-up," said Campbell. "It was a cool job, but it didn't work."

"A cool job?" she echoed.

"Haines was pushed over the edge of the rock. No doubt about that. The fellow that pushed him over then went to a telephone and rang up and said that he was Haines, confessed that he had committed the murder, and said that he was going to commit suicide. He told us the stuff then, about Willett hiring him for the Pollok job."

"But how *could* anyone . . . ," said the girl.

"Here was where this killer slipped up," said Campbell. "Between the time when he shoved Slogger over the cliff and the time he telephoned, about a half hour went by. The point is that the Slogger had been dead at least half an hour when we got the telephone call. It was another man who telephoned in his name."

"How *could* it be?" cried Rose Taylor.

She was growing pale. Her eyes were staring.

"I'm telling you the straight of it. The medical examiner doesn't make mistakes about the length of time a body lies dead."

Campbell grew warm with friendliness. He patted her sleek young shoulder gently. "I just wanted to tell you to watch O'Rourke. He's mean. He's terribly mean. What I think is that he wants to mix *you* up in this Haines murder. That's absurd. I know how crazy it is. But I wanted to tell you. I've got to go now. Good luck to you, Rose. And look out for O'Rourke. Dangerous fellow. Irish, and damned dangerous."

He got out of the place and, ten minutes later, was telephoning O'Rourke.

"Rose Taylor looked up Haines not long ago. A strange man went to see the Slogger in the boarding house he lived in and still kept a room in when he was with Willett. Could Willett have been the man who went to see Haines? Most likely.

"I've just left Rose Taylor, and I've put on two of the boys to shadow her. I've warned her that you're against her and think she had a hand in the Haines murder. I've told her that Haines could not have committed suicide. It was a killing. I've told her so much that she thinks you know everything."

O'Rourke spoke over the wire for the first time.

"What's the matter with you? Crazy? Why would you spill the beans to that rat of a girl?"

"Because I think she'll run to her partner in this business, whoever her partner is. And the shadows I've put on the job will take us to something, perhaps. If we don't get a good lead out of this before long, I *am* going crazy. There are three dead men, now, and they're all on one trail. I *am* going nutty."

"You were born that way," said O'Rourke, and rang off.

32

❖

"Rose Taylor Springs
a Trap"

Sergeant O'Rourke lighted a cigar and smoked it through from end to butt before his telephone interrupted his frowning thoughts again.

The voice said, "Sergeant Campbell or O'Rourke, please."

"O'Rourke speaking."

"Rose Taylor left her place with two packed suitcases, twenty minutes after Campbell went out of her apartment. She headed straight downtown. She's now at the dock of the French Line buying a ticket for Europe."

"Hold everything!" said O'Rourke. "I'll be there on the jump."

It was one of those summer fogs. The streets were adrip with it. It brought the heat down and breathed it into one's face. It was a day when sick people look out of the window and die of despair, glad to leave this smothered earth. O'Rourke went through the waiting line with his badge. A thin little man with a pointed face came up and walked behind him.

"Where?" said O'Rourke.

"Gangway for second class."

"Rose is a thrifty gal," said O'Rourke. "She wouldn't spend more than she had to. Not for silly things like steamship tickets. Anybody meet her?"

"Nobody I could spot. But she's expecting someone. You can spot her away over there, walking up and down."

"Is her luggage on board?"

"Yes."

"Fade out, then, Bennett."

"Sure," said Bennett, and was gone.

O'Rourke sifted through the crowd and took up his place in a far corner of the vast barnlike building, sitting on a pile of boxes. He took out a pocketknife, sliced a sliver of wood from the box, and began to whittle from it long, translucent shavings.

Rose Taylor was no longer walking up and down. She was standing still. Now she was starting forward. And through the shift of the crowd, O'Rourke saw Jacqueline Barry coming.

He blinked. He was ready to expect anything, but not that. There was no use being closer. He could see clearly enough the cordiality of that greeting. He could see the hand of Jacqueline open her purse, slip into it, press something into the hand of Rose Taylor.

That was when they shook hands in farewell.

He remembered the scene at the Barry house, that night, the cold, fixed staring of the eyes, the fury of Rose Taylor, the savagery with which she had attacked the other girl.

O'Rourke, watching Jacqueline out of sight through the throng again, arose with a sigh. He felt old and weary and weak. Perhaps he knew a little bit about men, but women he never would pretend to judge again. The sourness grew in him. From this moment forward he never would trust even his own wife.

Jacqueline Barry. Jacqueline with the clear, clean, cold, disdainful green eyes. Jacqueline cordially taking the hand of lovely Rose Taylor . . . and leaving something in the grip of the girl!

Rose had disappeared up the gangplank. But it was not hard for O'Rourke to follow her to the upper deck where she stood at the rail and looked down through the mist at the swirl of faces along the dock. O'Rourke touched her shoulder.

As she turned, he watched the blink of her eyes. She recovered instantly from the stroke of fear.

"Ah, Sergeant O'Rourke," she said. "Nice to see you again. Come to wish me bon voyage? I didn't know that you covered shipping."

"Come with me, Rose," he said. "I'll carry your purse for you."

"Come with you?" said Rose. "But . . . Mr. O'Rourke!"

"Sorry," he said.

"But I can't come. The ship is sailing in just a few moments and I. . . ."

"What's in the little twist of paper that you put into your purse?" he asked.

"I don't know," said Rose. "I mean. . . ."

He took the purse from her faintly resisting hand. He opened it and pulled out the paper twist which had glimmered as it passed from the palm of Jacqueline Barry to that of Rose Taylor. Inside the paper were simply two unset emeralds, big, lustrous, flawless to the first glance. O'Rourke looked at the girl.

"A sailing gift," said Rose Taylor.

"From whom?" asked O'Rourke.

Only for an instant did her eyes linger on his in doubt before she answered, "From Mr. Jeffrey Morrison, Mr. O'Rourke."

"And Morrison sent Jacqueline Barry as his messenger?" asked O'Rourke.

She did not blush. Her eyes opened a little wider in plain terror. Then they squinted a bit.

"Come with me, Rose," he said.

"Have you a warrant for my arrest?" she demanded suddenly.

"In this purse of yours I have all I want," he said. "Shall I ask the cop on the pier to take a look at the emeralds you're carting away with you? Want him to ask questions about where you got them?"

For a long moment she stared at the sergeant. Then she nodded.

"I'll come," she said.

When they were in the car, O'Rourke said, cheerfully, "From the first time I saw you, beautiful, I always had an idea that you and I would ride to jail together. I dunno why I had the idea. Pretty is as pretty does. Maybe that was the hunch I was playing. And you were too damned pretty, Rose."

She said nothing.

"But what boiled me the most," said the sergeant, "was the way you went for Willett."

"Are you taking me to jail?" she asked.

"I am, darling," said O'Rourke.

"Is it true that they cut a girl's hair short when she goes to prison?" asked Rose Taylor.

"Not always," said O'Rourke.

She sighed. "Are you really going to keep me in jail?"

"Yes," said O'Rourke.

"I'm glad of that," she said.

"Are you? Well, I'm damned!" said O'Rourke.

"Because if you were to send me away from it, I'd be dead in thirty minutes," said Rose.

"What the devil are you talking about?" asked O'Rourke.

She shook her head.

"Who are you afraid of now, Rose?" he demanded.

"Do you think I'd give it a name?" she asked, shuddering.

He stared at her from the corner of his eye, curiously. Perhaps her emotion was real. But he would not trust it. So long as he lived, he never again would believe what his eyes told him about women.

33

❖

"Three Visitors"

I t was a small room, far down. The shadows from the big
buildings around never allowed the sun to touch at its
barred window. And the single electric light that hung from
the ceiling threw strange shadows.

Campbell said, "What did you do with her?"

"They're taking her history, and drawing it out long," answered O'Rourke.

"The Barry girl at the dock, eh?" murmured Campbell, and
tapped the tips of his fingers rapidly, nervously on the surface of
the desk.

The telephone gave a feeble tinkle. Campbell answered.

"Jeffrey Morrison is just going to the Flytrap to see Willett,"
said a voice. "Shall we leave them alone?"

"Leave everybody alone. Let everybody have a chance to
talk to him peacefully. We'll have our ear in, down here."

"What if one of these birds tries to pass something to Willett?"

"We can search him afterwards."

"It's your funeral, Sergeant. The chief wouldn't like this if it
got noised around."

A hollow voice sounded inside the little room. It came from
a metal horn with a spreading mouth.

"Hello, Willett."

"There's Morrison now," whispered Campbell.

"Ah, Jeffrey Morrison," said the voice of Willett, somewhat
less hollow in sound through the horn. "What brought you
down here? A chance to gloat a little?"

"No, no," said Morrison. "My God, no, Willett. I came out of a friendly feeling. . . . How does it feel . . . ? I mean, the bars all around. . . ."

"They've done me proud," said Willett. "You see, they've put me in this little block of cells all by myself. That keeps me from organizing a jailbreak. Oh, these fellows have a lot of brains."

"I wanted to tell you, Willett, that I never suspected that you were the man. I thought you were innocent all the way through."

"That's kind of you."

"Barry was a snake."

"There was poison in him, all right," agreed Willett.

"Had you figured it out, or was it just impulse?"

"Just impulse," said Willett.

"You had to get your hands on his scrawny throat, eh?"

"I thought it was a certain pull that I used," answered Willett.

"Well . . . I felt the same way. I felt the same way that same night," said Morrison.

"You've been brooding on this thing," said Willett.

"God knows that I have reason enough to brood! I want to know if there's anything that I can do for you?"

"Not a thing," said Willett. "You look bad, Morrison. You need a few drinks and then a long sleep."

"Sleep?" groaned Morrison. "I'll never sleep again."

"How much did pretty little Rose get under your skin?"

"She's a rat!" said Morrison.

"God made her the way she is," said Willett. "You run along and take care of yourself."

"There's nothing I can do, Willett?"

"Nothing, Morrison. Thanks again."

"My God, how wonderfully you bear up!" said Morrison.

The telephone jingled softly again.

"Morrison has just left the Flytrap. John Telford is next," said the voice.

"Give him plenty of elbow room," said Campbell. "Grab

Morrison and put him in a room by himself. Don't explain anything. Just show him into a room and lock the door on him."

"Right-o," said the voice.

O'Rourke muttered, "You want to sweat Morrison a little?"

"We've got him softened up. We could reach into him with our bare hands and lift the heart out of him, now," said Campbell.

"That's the way you like to have 'em, isn't it?" asked O'Rourke. "But I think Morrison can tell us something more. Hush . . . here goes Telford and Willett. This ought to be good. Who else is coming to see Willett?"

"Jacqueline Barry. She's telephoned to make the appointment. She'll be right along."

The voice of Telford came smooth and deep. "Dick, I wonder if you'll forgive me for coming down here like this?"

Willett made no answer. After the ugly pause Telford's voice said, "I've been thinking it over since I read about your arrest. I've tried to be glad that this happened to you, Dick. But I can't be glad. I've spent a good many years hating you. Perhaps I've done the hating so long that a big chunk of my life would be missing if you were gone out of it. Can you understand that?"

"Are you getting sentimental?" asked Willett.

"You'd call it that, perhaps. The fact is, we've known each other for a long time, Dick."

"We have," said Willett, "and I've never known any good about you."

"Haven't you?" asked Telford, sadly. "Well, perhaps not much. But I've come down here to offer you my hand and my help . . . to bury the old grudge and see what I can do to make up for lost time. I've come to be your friend, Dick, if you'll let me!"

"Have you?" said Willett. "You'd take me for a friend, when you think that I'm a murderer of old Barry?"

"Dick, a man can be tempted. I know that. God forgive me if I judge anyone harshly from now on."

"You talk like the real Christian," said Willett. "Like a real early Christian, Johnnie. Now let me tell you something that will change your mind. I planted the clues that pointed to you. I changed the lamp shades. I pulled on the pajamas and lay in the bed. I remade everything and put it in good order . . . just good enough for a detective with half an eye to see that something was wrong. I burned the broken shade, and I threw the wire into the brush in front of your house. I laid every clue to point to you, John. Now let's see how much forgiveness there is in you!"

"You hated me, Dick, didn't you?" said Telford. "Well, I don't blame you. It doesn't make me angry, Dick. It makes me damned sad. I don't care what you've done, I'm offering you my hand. Will you take it?"

"I'll see myself damned first," said Willett.

"Ah, that's too bad," said Telford. "There's nothing for me to say but good-bye. I hate this, Dick. It tears something in my heart."

"Ah, to hell with you," said Willett.

A MOMENT LATER the telephone said to Campbell, "Miss Barry is going in. All right?"

"All right," said Campbell.

Then he added to O'Rourke, "What did you think of that?"

"I don't know what to think," said O'Rourke. "It wasn't anybody, so far as I can see. Have we got to go back to the suicide idea? Certainly Telford didn't have a hand in the job."

"What about Willett?" demanded Campbell. "I tell you I've known all along. Did you hear him, just now? I'm asking you to think of the nerve of a man who'll stay in the house of a dead man and arrange matters the way he did. Nerve? There's not a nerve in his body. Not a nerve, I tell you! He could murder twenty people, and then laugh about it."

201

"Be still," said O'Rourke. "There goes the girl. . . . Zow-ie! . . . ! Listen to her, will you?"

He whispered to keep his voice from covering the words that came rushing into the room, half musical, half weeping, so that a disembodied sorrow seemed to be breathing before them.

"She loves him!" murmured Campbell. "Now damn me white and black, I never suspected that."

"By what a female says, you never can tell," muttered O'Rourke.

"Listen again, you fool!" murmured Campbell. "Listen to the way her voice sings a song over him. . . . By the living God, she's askin' him to kiss her through the bars, and. . . ."

". . . and he won't!" whispered O'Rourke. "Can you come over that?"

"The low, murderin', hard-hearted devil!" said Campbell.

"She's still cryin'," said O'Rourke.

"You're looking soppy yourself," murmured Campbell.

"It's that *she* could be carryin' on like this!" said O'Rourke. "And I thought she was the chilled steel . . . ! My God, what do I know about women . . . ? Nothing!"

"Hush!" said Campbell. He began to repeat the words that came mourning through the room, whispering them softly.

Then he was silent. For a long moment he was still. At last the telephone rang.

"Miss Barry's just gone out. Here's a funny thing, Sergeant. She's pretty badly broken down. She passed Telford in the cor-ridor. He was waiting for her there. He says, 'Jacqueline, what in Heaven's name is the matter?' And she says, big and clear, so's half a dozen of us could hear: 'John, I love him. I'll always love him . . . and they're going to kill him . . . oh, God help me!' Like that she says it. And she goes on and leaves Telford standing straight up and knocked for a row of loops. . . . Listen, Sergeant. Telford wants to go back and see Willett again."

"Let him go," said Campbell.

He turned to O'Rourke.

"It's coming kind of fast, ain't it?" he asked.

"If she cut off Telford . . . then it wasn't simply playacting when she was talking with Willett," said O'Rourke.

"Playacting? You're still wiping your eyes, you soggy fool!"

"The theater's always kind of too much for me when people get to saying good-bye to one another," said O'Rourke.

"There they go again," murmured Campbell.

Through the loud speaker the voice of Willett was saying, "Here comes the bad penny back again. What do you want this time, Telford?"

"I want . . . ," began Telford.

Then the voice was cut off.

"The wire's broken!" exclaimed Campbell. "What in hell is going to pop up there now?"

He caught up the telephone.

34

❖

"Murderer's World"

Over the telephone, Campbell was rattling his words, "Tell the guards at the Flytrap to break right in!" O'Rourke snatched the receiver violently away and shouted, "O'Rourke speaking. Tell the guards to turn Willett out of his cell and bring him with Telford down to the room where Morrison is now. Stop Jacqueline Barry and bring her to the same place. Get Rose Taylor there, too. . . . On the run, all of you! On the run! Willett and Telford first or you'll have a double killing right here in the jail. . . ."

He slammed up the receiver and sat back with a groan of excitement.

"What the devil do you mean by all this?" asked Campbell, angrily.

"I've got a hunch . . . a hunch . . . a hunch!" shouted O'Rourke. "Come on, Angus. Get in at the finish. This is where the race ends for somebody."

It was a long, narrow, cold, dark room. It was the shape of a large coffin. Instead of one light hanging from the ceiling, it had two. In the two patches of electric light, badly needed in spite of the sun that glinted on a wall beyond the window, they had gathered Rose Taylor, Morrison, Jacqueline Barry, Telford, and Willett with manacles on his wrists. Two policemen were there. It was on this scene that the sergeants entered.

"Morrison, stop your groaning," said O'Rourke. "You're

not in the electric chair yet. . . . Barney, what did you find in the Flytrap?"

One of the policemen said, "Both of them were hanging onto the bars and glaring at each other through 'em. Their faces were inches apart. They'd of been at each other's throats, in another second, right through the bars."

"You're wrong," said Willett. "I don't use bare hands on a man with a gun. Not if I can help it."

"Not carrying concealed weapons, are you, Mr. Telford?" asked O'Rourke.

"Certainly not," said Telford.

"He lies," said Willett. "He was fingering a gun when he came back to talk to me the second time. He was so sour that he couldn't help putting his hand on the gun. If you can't believe me, search him."

"Absurd!" said Telford.

"We're gonna play this safe, absurd or not," said O'Rourke. "Mr. Telford, just hold out your arms while I go through you. Sorry, but a little. . . ."

"Search me! I'll see you damned first," said Telford.

He was near the door and now he jerked it open suddenly. O'Rourke, astonished, was too slow to intervene. But Willett had leaped the moment Telford spoke. His hands were fastened together. He swung them up like a club above his head and struck Telford with the hard weight of the handcuffs.

Telford crashed into the corner. Three pairs of hands had secured him before he could stir again. And Barney was shoving the muzzle of a revolver into Willett's stomach.

Neither of the girls had cried out. Morrison was sitting up in his chair, agape. His confinement in the coffin-like room had melted away the last nerve-strength in his body and his soul. He trembled as he stared.

"It's all right, officer," said Willett. "I think I tapped the right wire, that time. He's not hurt."

Telford was lifted to his feet. He was swaying a little and a thin trickle of blood ran down his face from the cut on his head where the steel had struck home. Sergeant O'Rourke was holding in hand the big automatic which he had just taken from Telford's clothes.

Willett said, quietly, "That's a Kelmsford, I think . . . if that makes any difference to you, Sergeant."

O'Rourke said, as he examined the gun, "This used to belong to you, Morrison. Did you give it to Telford?"

"No," said Morrison. "I. . . ."

"What do you mean, Morrison?" demanded Telford.

"Why . . . yes, yes!" stammered Morrison. "I must have given it to him. I seem to remember now. Yes, I do remember that. . . ."

"Stop lying!" commanded Campbell. He was staring at Telford.

"Barney," said O'Rourke, "put up your gun and don't be a damned fool. Go and take this gun to the ballistics office. And find out if it shoots the same sort of bullet as that which smashed into the head of Sidney Pollok. Go ahead and make it quick."

Telford said, "It was a foolish thing for me to carry that weapon, Sergeant Campbell. But the fact is that there has been danger around me. . . ."

"The fact is," murmured Willett, "that I tagged you just in time, Johnnie. I think you'll stay 'It' till you go up Salt Creek."

"I wish to make a statement . . . ," said Telford.

"Touch and go, Johnnie," said Willett. "It was a near thing, if only you'd been able to get along without that rod. But when a man has the taste for murder, he has to have the tools he likes around him, isn't that so?"

Telford glared at him.

"Let him talk, Mr. Willett," said Campbell.

O'Rourke said, "He doesn't need to talk. He'll burn for three murders, Campbell. And pretty little Rose will burn for helping him with the last one. Is that right, Rose? Did he pay you enough hard cash for helping him to bump over Slogger Haines?"

"The Slogger?" cried Willett. "You mean that the Slogger has been killed?"

"I had nothing to do with it!" exclaimed Rose.

O'Rourke lifted a hand and pointed slowly at her, as though he were aiming a gun, "You were seen the night of his death walking. . . ."

"Ah!" cried Rose.

"Steady!" said Telford. "Don't let them bluff you, Rose."

"You were seen . . . ," said O'Rourke, solemnly.

"But I didn't do it!" cried the girl. "I was only near enough to watch *him* do it!"

Telford, after looking a moment toward her, turned his glance to Willett and stared steadily. The rest of the world had vanished from his mind.

"Get the handcuffs off Willett," said O'Rourke over his shoulder. "We'll need them for Telford, I think."

Willett said, "It was the last touch that turned the trick, Johnnie. If you hadn't come back to gloat a bit, I never would have seen that gun in the back of your mind. . . . But damn you, did you kill poor Slogger Haines?"

Telford said, "It seems as though some strange combination of circumstances, including the momentary possession of a gun belonging to Mr. Morrison, and an hysterical girl. . . ."

"You can't get me into it," screamed out Morrison. "Sergeant Campbell! Listen to me! Sergeant O'Rourke, for God's sake, listen to me! I had two of those guns. I wish to God I never bought them . . . ! I had two. And one of them was missing on the twenty-first, when Telford came to my office. I never saw it again, and. . . ."

"Morrison," said Telford, "I'm going to smash. . . ."

He stopped himself.

"Don't look at Morrison," said Willett. "Look at me, Johnnie. Morrison hasn't done anything."

As though compelled by the command, Telford turned back to glare at Willett.

"Try me once more, Johnnie. I think I could crack your

skull for you this time. . . . You're going to burn for poor Slogger Haines and for Pollok. It doesn't matter, now, if you don't burn for the thing you didn't do."

"Go ahead, Mr. Willett," said O'Rourke. "What thing didn't he do?"

"He didn't murder Barry, except morally," said Willett. "If you don't mind, I'm going to get Miss Barry out of here . . . unless you think you have some further call on me? Jacqueline, shall we leave?"

He went across the room and took the arm of the girl. Only when she was touched, she showed the effect of the terrible shock she had sustained. As his hand fell on her arm, her head dropped back a little as though she were about to faint. She recovered herself immediately.

"I'm not going to leave until I know whatever I *can* know," she said.

Sergeant Campbell said, "Willett, we can't hold you for the Pollok business. The medical examiner has proved that Haines was dead at the same time that the voice rang us up and announced that it was Haines speaking and that you had hired him to kill Pollok."

"That would be good old Johnnie, again," said Willett. "Your ballistic boy will tell you that Telford slammed the bullet into Pollok."

Campbell went on, "Is it true that on the night of the twenty-second you were sitting at one time smoking a cigarette and watching the body of Barry swing back and forth from the balcony?"

"Perfectly true," said Willett. "And it's true that afterwards I planted the clues pointing to Telford. Whether it was suicide or not, the moral guilt was Telford's. He'd put Barry in such a corner, with his lies about the district attorney's investigation, that Barry was ready to kill himself, or to be killed. When I came back from telephoning, I found him dead, hanging by the neck. I untied and retied his shoes. I arranged things in the bedroom to make it seem as though he'd been strangled when he was in bed, the bed remade, and the body put up on the balcony the way it was found. Jacqueline didn't come back and find me there. That was just a handsome lie to save my neck. Matter of fact, most of the yarn that dear little Rose told that evening was entirely true."

Rose Taylor, who had been staring constantly at Jacqueline and Willett with a strange look, suddenly buried her face in her hands and began to weep violently.

"She pities herself," said Campbell.

"It's a funny thing that even a hard-boiled piece of flint like Rosie, there, has to cry when you make her pity herself. She pities herself because for once in her life she told the truth . . . O'Rourke, look out!"

Telford, all this while, never had withdrawn his glare from the face of Willett. He was being firmly pinioned by either arm and the handcuffs, which had been removed from the wrists of Willett, were now taken toward him. In addition to these precautions, Officer Barney steadily pointed a service Colt, forty-five caliber, at the midsection of the prisoner. In spite of that unlucky environment, Telford made one vast final effort.

A swing of his leg drove the heel against Barney's shin and almost broke his leg. Barney's hand instinctively jerked under the excess of agony and the gun exploded. Telford, jerking the weapon out of Barney's nerveless hand, cracked the heel of it a glancing blow on the head of the second policeman, and then turned it on Willett.

He had needed only a fifth of a second to catch hold of the weapon. He had another moment to fire pointblank at Willett before O'Rourke from one side and Barney from the other dived at him. Twice he pulled the trigger, then he buckled to his knees as O'Rourke lunged in and bore him down. He collapsed as though there were no strength of blood or breath in him.

Jacqueline had tried to get between the thundering gun and Willett. Now it was he who caught her in his arms.

"I'm all right," he called to her, "but you, Jacqueline? Did he hit you? Has he hurt you?"

She lay back with her head drooping over the hook of his arm.

"No!" she whispered. "But I thought that was the end. I thought that I'd only have one glimpse of Heaven, and then the door would be slammed in my face."

O'Rourke, rising from the prostrate body of Telford, fairly hurled himself on the two of them.

"Are y'all right, Willett?" he asked.

"Hell, O'Rourke," said Willett, "the kind of bullets you fellows have in those guns simply bounce off a real man. . . . Jacqueline, tell me again . . . you're not hurt? He couldn't have missed us both."

"A dying man don't shoot straight," said the cold voice of Campbell. "Telford is passing out on us. There'll be no electric chair for him, after all."

Telford's voice said, in a perfectly calm and easy manner, "Get my head up a little. I want to look at things that I'm leaving."

Jacqueline suddenly was on the floor. She braced up his head and shoulders on her lap and in her arms. There was no power in him. He seemed paralyzed completely, except that his eyes were clear and his voice perfectly steady. The bullet from Barney's gun had ripped straight through his body from side to side. The blood kept pouring.

Campbell said, "What about Rose Taylor? Will you talk about her?"

And Telford answered, "She's not worth talking about. . . . I haven't any time. But everybody in hell knows that I killed Barry, so you might as well know it, too. . . . Where's that fat-faced swine, Morrison? He started everything. He couldn't be content to bleed Barry little by little till his meat was white. He gouged in so deep that Barry began to notice something. When Barry called at the office on the twenty-first, he knew things were wrong. Before he'd finished talking with Morrison, he knew that I'd had my fingers in the honey. He turned on a fine power of hate for Morrison.

"Barry only wanted a bit more evidence before he sent me

to jail. That was why I pulled the district attorney's fake investigation on him. He had to die that night, suicide or murder. The next day, he would have found out that I'd been collecting some extra profits from him. . . . Willett guessed the whole story. He knew what had happened. He faked the stuff to point to me, but he was right. I got you to go to him, Jacqueline, and try to soften him up a little. But when you reported that Barry wouldn't soften, I knew that something had to be done. I went up to see him. He was sour. He began giving me hell. I started to pull the curtains together. I was so angry that I pulled the cord right off the rod. I stood there with the cord in my hand. Barry sat in a chair with his back to me, still snarling. He'd see in the morning whether I were an honest man or not. It was a wide open chance. The cord there in my hand talked to me and told me what to do. Afterwards I draped him like a flag without a country from the balcony. . . ."

"We had enough stuff on you to hang you twice," said Campbell. "The third job hardly mattered."

"That's right," said Telford. "I'm almost sorry to cheat you boys, after the way you've sweated."

Jacqueline said, "John, stop talking. Has anyone a drop of brandy or whiskey . . . ? Here, take a swallow of this. Don't talk, John, any more . . . unless you want to say different things."

"It's not a bad way to pass out. Used to think of lying like this with my head in your lap. But that never happened. You never gave a real damn about me, Jacqueline, and that forced me to love your money. You know. I still hoped that I'd touch your heart, one day, and then I found out this afternoon that you love Willett. Willett, when I had him steered for the electric chair, d'you see? The irony of that did me in. Going to him when he was about to die. That knocked me dizzy. I had to rush back and damn him a little. And that was what made me reach for the gun without thinking about it. Between the two of you, you did me in . . . you and Willett."

"John, talk about something else. There *are* other things to talk about."

211

"Childhood memories, and the virtues that I might have attained?" said Telford. He was stone-white. His lips looked stone-color, too. But his smile made his face beautiful. "I wasn't meant for that sort of chatter, Jacqueline," he said. "Do you want to know when I had my happiest times?"

He kept looking up at her, rolling back his eyes, smiling.

He said, "When I got the cord around Barry's neck and twisted it. He sort of leaped up in the chair. He was amazingly spry. He turned his head around and saw me. I gave another twist. The curtain cord turned into an electric wire. A joy came up through it into my hands and my heart. I never had lived an instant before that. . . . Afterwards, I was entirely calm. I told myself that I ought to hurry a little, but still I took my time. As I remember, I was humming when I carried him up the stairs to the balcony. He lay like a child in my arms. A little, old, prematurely white child. I dropped him over the balcony. I wondered if the curtain cord would break, because that would have spoiled things. But it held. The knots came taut with a slight creak. That was all. I went down and looked things over. Everything seemed all right. So I went home. I was happy enough to sing. I *did* sing."

"You got the taste then, didn't you?" asked O'Rourke.

"After I felt Barry turn limp under the twist of the cord, the days were pretty empty for me, except that I began right away to figure how I could do you in, Willett. That would have been the crowning moment. . . . But take Pollok. He didn't know enough to bother me a great deal. I could have shut his mouth with a little dirty money . . . Jacqueline's money. But there was the temptation. When he came with the threats, I told him I'd bring him the money. I had it with me, too. But when I got into his room, I remembered the gun in my pocket. I thought how easy the thing would be. And it *was* easy. Nothing pleasanter ever happened than the way he slipped down out of his chair. A woman's voice was squeaking over the wire.

"I hung the receiver up. I hated to leave the place. I felt a peace in that room. I went out slowly, almost too slowly for safety. Afterwards, when I had the clever idea about the Slogger, I used dear little Rose . . . don't turn so white, sweetheart. I'm not going to tell everything. You stay up here among things and carry on the good work. Have your own fun. What broke me up was sheer luck. My car was half a block away. I ran to it. A tire had gone flat. I changed the thing. If I'd used the brain, I would have run on the flat tire. Then you would have had the telephone call within fifteen minutes of the death of the Slogger, and your medical examiner couldn't have been exact enough to make the difference count in a law court. . . . Think of that, Willett. You owe your life to the changing of a tire. You ought to change a tire every day you live. When you get bored, go out and change a tire. It will freshen things up for you. . . . Give me another pull at that flask, will you . . . ? Ah."

Willett leaned above him.

"Barry and Pollok didn't matter. They didn't add up to much," he said. "But the Slogger. How did you feel about the poor Slogger? There was an honest man, Johnnie."

"I'll tell you what," said Telford. "When he dropped over the fence, I watched him whirling in the air and wondered why he didn't yell out. I counted the times he bumped the rocks, and then the slam of his body on the pavement. And I wish that I'd been down there to look at the wreck. . . . Do you think you'll get penitence out of me? You've had all the luck in a lump. You've won the game in the last five minutes, but my God, I've had the fun of running up and down the field! I've had the. . . ."

His voice stopped. His body bent up into an arc as though he were trying to look more squarely into the face of Jacqueline. She bent over him. Gradually he relaxed. His half-opened eyes continued to study the nearest of the electric lights.

"That's all," said Campbell.

"The door opened. A policeman saluted and reported, "The ballistic report says that the same gun. . . ."

"Oh, back up," said O'Rourke. "That's stale news. . . . What's the matter, Rose? Are you sick?"

213

"Can I go?" said Rose.

"Yeah. Get out and stay out."

AFTERWARDS, O'Rourke said, "It's all pretty clear. But why did Jacqueline Barry give Rose the jewels?"

"Anything to get her out of the country," answered Campbell. "She was afraid that what Rose had to say might be the knife stuck in the back of Willett at the trial. And maybe she was right."

"But why did Rose want to run?"

"She knew what Telford had done. Barry . . . Pollok . . . Haines. When she heard that Haines's murder was known, she decided to jump, partly for fear the law would get her, but mostly for fear of Telford.

"Did you see his eyes when he was making his last talk? Maybe she saw the same look in them before. It was a good reason for making a gal jump for Europe and parts East."

ONLY AN HOUR LATER the inspector was saying, ". . . a case so difficult, involved, with suspicion so widely scattered, that it seemed impossible to localize the guilt. But the guilt was finally placed on the right shoulders. By brain work and the encountering of danger; by dauntless courage, sagacity, perseverance, two men . . . working shoulder to shoulder . . . examples of quiet heroism and devoted loyalty, examples which I want to hold up in front of all you men, enabled the crimes to be brought home on the head of the wrongdoer. . . . I want you men of the force to see what friendship and an unswerving affection, built up through years of intimacy, has accomplished on behalf of the law. . . . Sergeants Campbell and O'Rourke, kindly stand up and face the men in this room. . . ."

They were out in the corridor, afterwards, hot and bothered. O'Rourke said, "I'm gonna go back and tell the truth. It wasn't us that got the dope. It was Willett that collected most of the proof . . . and nearly got the electric chair for a reward."

214

"He'll think you're talking with a small mouth. He'll think you're fishing," said Campbell. "Take everything you can get and put it in your pocket. It'll help you when you're up for drunkenness, neglect of duty, and the taking of graft. . . . I wash my hands of you. I'll never. . . ."

"What a fool you are!" said O'Rourke. "No matter what the dumb inspector thinks, everybody on the force knows that it's the Irish brain that turns the trick. Everybody laughs when you go by; everybody winks when they see you, Campbell. Why don't you wake up and see how the boys are laughing? If half your weight was made of diamonds I wouldn't have you for a gift."

WILLETT SAID, "Why not slow down a little? Or maybe you think this is a straight road?"

"I want to get inside a new horizon," answered Jacqueline. "Then we can slow down and . . . well, and get ready for a new start."

"Then drive like the devil till we get on the other side of that hill."

"The brown one?"

"No, the blue one," said Willett. "There's a new world on the other side of that."

The car gathered speed and rushed forward as if it knew this was so.